I0738710

A Fable of Freedom

& other stories

Robert Villanueva

The Heartland Review Press/Elizabethtown, KY

Acknowledgements

"Falling From Grace" was first published in the print magazine *The Heartland Review*, Fall 2002.

"A Stranger's Place" was first published in the Fall 2002 issue of the print magazine, *The Heartland Review* and was the June 2006 Best Fiction Piece winner for the e-publication Ourecho.com.

"A Scent Like Daphne" was first published in the e-zine *The Summerset Review*, Spring 2006, and later selected for inclusion in the first print edition of *The Summerset Review*, March 2007.

"Act Like No One's Watching" was first published in the e-zine *The Flask Review*, Issue 8, May 2007, and later the print magazine *The Binnacle*, Spring 2007.

"A Short Stretch of Road" was first published in print in *Glassfire Anthology*, December 2007.

"Feathered Friend" was first published in the print anthology *Return of the Raven*, April 2009.

"A Dark and Fearsome Beast" was first published in the e-anthology *Florilegium*, November 2009.

Printed in the USA
1st edition, 2018

The Heartland Review Press
600 College Street Road
Elizabethtown, KY 42701

theheartlandreview@gmail.com
http://www.theheartlandreview.com

ISBN: 978-0-9996868-0-5

$14.95

Contents

A Fable of Freedom
& other stories

A SHORT STRETCH OF ROAD

Naturally, Roger and Carla thought their retired parents had flipped their lids. Maybe, Carla thought, Mom had watched a motivational episode of Oprah after overdosing on Ginseng. Dad must have started his model ship building again, Roger concluded, and perhaps he forgot the importance of proper ventilation when using that kind of glue.

"Well? Say something," Beverly prompted, drawing her half-filled cup of coffee to her lips, then setting it back down with precise care.

Roger and Carla didn't move. Their mouths froze somewhere between smiles and words.

"We've traumatized them, Walt," Beverly said, leaning along the edge of the dining room table toward her husband.

"Maybe we should call 9-1-1 or something," Walt mused, shifting his eyes to his wife without moving his head. "Or maybe we should call their spouses; I bet Tom and Elaine could snap them out of it."

Carla broke out of her trance with a start. She managed a short laugh.

"Oh, Mom and Dad, for a minute I thought you were serious," Carla put a hand on her throat and let her body go limp. She smiled at her parents, never taking her eyes off them, afraid if she did it would allow them the privilege of contradicting her.

"Oh, you're joking!" Roger said, falling back against his chair, a ragged chuckle escaping his lips. "You guys had me going, too!"

Walt and Beverly turned to each other. Walt shrugged, and Beverly grimaced.

"Are you two on crack or something?" Beverly pressed the knuckles of both hands on her hips. "We told you months ago about our plans to leave Ordinary and travel the country. We've finally worked out the details."

"You're serious?" Roger said, stretching out the question and dropping his voice.

"Oh, Roger, of course they're not," Carla said, not allowing her parents a chance to respond.

Walt threw his hands up. He leaned back in his chair and shook his head.

"I take it you're going to be in denial about this?" Beverly said.

"Oh, Mom," Carla said, standing up. She began clearing the lunch dishes from the table and began washing them.

"What about you?" Beverly raised her eyebrows at her son. She ignored the way the clattering of dishes and swish of body movement at the kitchen sink abruptly stopped. But she saw Roger's attention lock onto something in that direction before he answered his mother.

"What am I supposed to think?" Roger said. He looked back and forth between his parents. "Dad, you haven't by any chance started building model ships again?"

"Oh, for Pete's sake, son! You forget to ventilate once, and suddenly you're a glue-sniffing hippie!" Walt said. He grumbled something and rose from his chair. "I'm not going to argue. We're going, and that's that!"

Beverly stood up and patted her husband's arm before he marched toward the sliding glass door that opened into the back yard. He paused, looking out at his three grandchildren playing basketball on the small court.

"We'll be gone for three months," Beverly said. "When we get back we'll go straight to our new house in Bardstown. We're having everything sent there. Wilma says this house should sell with no problem, and she's the best Realtor in town."

"They're on a long road," Walt muttered. He stood looking out the back door.

"Loreen's in the road?" Carla rushed to her father's side. "She knows she's supposed to stay inside the fence—"

"She's not in the road," Beverly said. She sipped the last of her coffee and made her way to the kitchen.

"I'm going to shoot some hoops with my grandchildren," Walt said. He stepped outside.

*　　*　　*

The dappled shade of the backyard cooled the June sunshine that burst out from behind the low, foamy clouds. Somewhere in the collage of elm and cedar leaves, mingling with the rising and falling buzz of the cicadas, robins called to each other between the echoes of children laughing as they played in other yards and nearby alleys.   Roger leaned back on the porch steps and listened to the life of Ordinary surge through the air. The ping of the basketball as it met the concrete court and the shouts and laughter of his own children, his niece and his parents blended in with the fullness of the town's voice. Roger smiled.

"This is ridiculous," Carla said, under her breath. She sat—her back straight and body tense—on an aluminum lawn chair she didn't seem to want to touch. "They can't be serious. We can't support their decision."

Roger rubbed the knees of his jeans and looked down. When he finally raised his eyes, he found he could not look at his older sister. Instead, he watched the game of horse in progress. Jason and Rachel laugh, and Roger found himself grinning.

Carla huffed at Roger's amusement, causing his smile to falter. He looked down at his tennis shoes.

"Maybe it's not such a big deal," he said. His voice wavered. "They're both healthy, smart—"

"Roger, look at them! They're too old for all of this!"

Roger remained silent. His eyes wandered over the garden, where a mixture of wildflowers stretched away from the soil. He looked at the trees, their mature arms reaching toward the blue and white firmament. He glanced at his family on the basketball court, their spirited bodies stepping off the earth in their play. Then he stared at Carla, her hands curled into fists under her arms.

4

Only when he heard his daughter's high-pitched squeal did Roger come out of his reverie. He had just enough time to brace himself as Rachel ran to him and draped her arms around his neck. She let herself fall against him, nearly knocking him off balance. Roger hugged his daughter with one arm and steadied himself with the other, planting his hand on the porch step.

"I won! I won!" Rachel squealed.

"Whew! She wore me out!" Walt said, wiping invisible sweat from his brow as he walked down the half court and plopped down beside them. "I must have lost ten pounds in sweat alone."

"Oh, Dad, you shouldn't get so worked up," Carla said, springing up from her chair. "I'm going to get some tea for everyone."

Without waiting for a response, Carla bounded up the back porch steps and into the house. Roger noticed the scowl on her face as she shot past him, and for some reason, he hugged Rachel tighter.

"They let me win," Rachel murmured. Her smile stretched wide.

"Nooooo? Really?"

Rachel paused, then gave her dad a dubious look. She pushed away from him and slapped his arm as if swatting a fly.

"Oh, Dad, of course they did!" Rachel said.

But Roger felt his heart stop. If he had closed his eyes at this last comment from his daughter he would have sworn it was his sister speaking. He suddenly felt scared.

"Too bad Elaine and Tom couldn't be here," Walt said. "I know Tom works his route Saturdays, but I thought Elaine didn't work weekends. Where is she?"

Roger turned to his father, his thoughts still jumbled and racing. He had to replay in his mind what his father had said.

"Elaine's conference ends this afternoon. She's driving back from Frankfort tonight."

"It takes a special person to be a social worker," Walt said. "But when your heart's in something it shows."

Roger saw the look on his father's face, like a map unfolding. He studied it and nodded. His dad winked at him.

"All right, everyone, drink up."

Carla placed the tray of drinks on the white cast iron table near the lawn chair she had sat on earlier. She motioned for everyone to move to the drinks after grabbing a glass for herself.

"Mommmmm! We're playing!" Loreen whined.

"And if you want to keep playing, you'll come and have a drink! Now come on. You need to keep yourself hydrated."

Loreen and her cousin Jason made their way to the drinks. Beverly continued shooting hoops. Loreen slouched and rolled her eyes as she picked up a glass of tea.

"If Dad were here he'd let us finish playing," Loreen grumbled.

"If your dad were here, I'd have to make him stop playing, too," Carla said. "Otherwise he'd get himself so hot and dried out he'd sound like an asthmatic donkey!"

Rachel and Jason sat near their father as they drank their tea, and Roger found himself wondering why he had grabbed a glass for himself when he really wasn't thirsty.

"Come on, Mom," Carla called. "Get yourself a glass of tea."

Beverly sank the shot and let out a whoop before turning to her daughter to reply. Her bangs clung to her forehead, pasted there like exclamation marks. Dark patches formed under her arms.

"I'm going for three in a row. That was number one."

"You can finish that later. Come on."

"Don't worry about me. I'll get something later."

"It's best that you stop, Mom."

"No, it's not. I may not get a chance later to finish this later," Beverly said, talking over her shoulder as she stood poised for her shot. "It looks like some storm clouds are trying to move in."

"It's not that important."

"It is to me."

Carla was silent. She held two glasses of tea.

"Dad, do we have to finish our tea before we play?" Jason looked at his sister as he asked the question. Rachel wiped the hair out of her eyes, waiting for her father's response.

Roger felt his father's eyes on him. He could see from the corner of his eye that Carla had half-turned toward him.

"No, Jason. You and Rachel can go on and play. But if you feel thirsty come back and drink some more, okay?"

"Okay," the siblings said in unison, as they shot off the porch steps and back onto the basketball court.

Roger could see the corners of his father's lips curl. But he could also feel a pair of eyes searing into him, like a magnifying glass over an insect.

*   *   *

"Do you suppose we shot ourselves in the foot?" Beverly waved from the front porch at the cars that drove away as she spoke.

"Maybe. But I don't care. We're still leaving in two weeks."

"Well, at least we'll get to enjoy the circus next Wednesday with our grand-kids before we leave. We're all supposed to go."

"That will be fine; we'll probably have most of our packing done by then. And maybe Carla will have lightened up by then, too."

Beverly smirked at her husband's comment. Then she turned away and tilted her head back, rubbing the nape of her neck.

Walt moved to one of the two chairs on the porch and eased into it. He picked up his pipe from the table and dug in his shirt pocket for the last of his tobacco.

"It gets dark too early now," Beverly said, standing at the porch railing. The orange sunset blazed around her, beyond her, cutting her silhouette in imperfect designs and incomplete shapes.

"No, it's right on time."

Smoke hung in the air around Walt like ocean foam, surrounding him, enveloping him. He thought he could hear the swooshing drone of traffic on 31-W, a sound that he could turn into crashing waves if he closed his eyes.

"You miss it, don't you?"

"What?"

"Helping build the roads that take people places."

"Yes. Of course. Yes."

"They're putting in a caution light on your short stretch of road, where it crosses Maple Street."

Walt smiled. He like the way she called it his stretch of road. He had supervised the construction of Magnolia Drive five years ago. It connected Main Street to Park Street granting a more direct access to Ordinary Town Park.

"Caution light," Walt mumbled. "That's what it needed. They wanted to make it a four-way stop."

"She won't let go," Beverly said.

"We knew that before we told her."

"She's a hard-working, responsible, practical woman," Beverly sighed. "Where did we go wrong?"

"I blame C-Span."

*　*　*

Beverly won the bet when Carla and Loreen showed up Monday morning. Walt had wagered that it would be Friday before Carla would attempt a stalling tactic.

For the first hour, Carla stayed away from the topic, even though evidence of the forthcoming departure of her parents was everywhere. Already boxes had been filled, sealed and labeled, and most of the knickknacks that usually decorated the living room, kitchen and dining room were nowhere to be found.

After sharing a breakfast of biscuits and gravy, Carla sent Loreen out back with her soccer ball to run practice drills. Then she settled down with a cup of coffee with Beverly as Walt excused himself to do more packing in the garage.

"I volunteered you to drive your van for vacation Bible school this summer!"

Beverly blinked. Her shoulders dropped.

"What's the matter with you?"

"What do you mean?"

"It's not going to work."

"I don't know what you mean, Mom. I thought you'd enjoy helping out the church with Bible school this summer before you and Dad take your vacation."

"You know we're leaving in two weeks," Beverly barked.

Carla dropped her eyes to her coffee cup. She scowled, as if disappointed, but she would not look at her mother.

"Oh, I must have misunderstood—"

"Misunderstood, my foot! You knew what you were doing, and it's not going to work."

Carla's jaw dropped, and her cheeks became flush. She glanced at her watch and looked around the room before turning her attention back to the

7

conversation.

"I must have been confused, Mom, that's all. But it's not like you couldn't put off that vacation."

Beverly folded her arms and sighed. She shook her head.

"You just won't give up, will you?"

Carla glanced at her watch again. Then she raised her coffee cup in front of her with both hands, as if she was putting up a shield between her and her mother.

"I think you're overreacting," Carla said.

"And I think you're crazier than a loon to volunteer me for something without asking me first. But then you knew I wouldn't agree to it."

"I just thought you'd want to help Judy out. I was talking to her yesterday at church, and she said she would have more kids at Bible school if they had transportation. She drives that little two-door, or else she would do it."

"You're just going to have to tell her what you've done and make other arrangements. I'm not letting you railroad me into this."

"But you should see the little Mathers girl with leukemia," Carla said, drawing her hands together and interlocking her fingers, as if approximating a gesture of pleading. "Her mother is legally blind and can't drive. All little Tina wants is to be able to do things like a normal child. And you'd be helping other kids, too."

"That's not the point—"

The doorbell rang before Beverly could finish her reproach. From where she sat, Beverly had a clear view of the open front door, but she could not see enough of the person standing on the porch to determine who it was. Glaring at her daughter with an intensity that was almost palpable, she stomped from the dining room to the living room.

Just before she reached the storm door, the visitor stepped into full view.

The sight of Judy Perkins stopped Beverly in her tracks. A bald child, no more than seven years old, clung to the hem of Judy's shorts, swaying behind her and beside her, like a brittle leaf on a fall tree, twisting in the wind.

*   *   *

Loreen tossed the ball up into the air in front of her, swinging at it with a clenched fist on its descent. The contact created a sharp slapping sound and sent the soccer ball hurtling across the lawn.

Walt stood at the basement steps that rose into the backyard, watching his granddaughter for a few minutes. He thought he could feel something behind each swipe Loreen took at her target. Each time she walked across the grass to retrieve the ball she appeared to be trying to get away from something rather than moving toward anything.

Even as Walt took a few steps in her direction, Loreen was oblivious to everything around her. She picked up the ball and stood at the chain link fence that enclosed the backyard, pushing the fingers of her free hand through the diamond-shaped openings and grasping the metal in a claw-like grip. Suddenly, she kicked the fence.

"Hey, sport," Walt called. "Need any help beating up that fence?"

Loreen snapped to attention, her face becoming flush as she faced her grandfather. She held his gaze for only a second before finding something on the ground to scrutinize.

"No, Grandpa." Her voice was thin as stretched cellophane.

"I don't mean to be a nosey Rosie, but is there anything you want to talk about?"

Walt had made his way to within a few feet of Loreen then stopped. He cocked his head, trying to read her face.

"No, Grandpa."

"Okay, Sweetie. Want to help me pack? I was just taking a break, but I could use a hand."

"Sure."

Loreen tossed the ball toward the back porch steps, but she didn't move from where she stood. Walt had started to turn but now hesitated.

"Grandpa?"

"Yes, Sweetie?"

"Are you and Grandma really going to drive around the country and then move to Bardstown?"

Walt took a deep breath. The bright sun fell across his face like a spotlight.

"Yes, Honey. But we won't be all that far from—"

"I think you should."

Walt drew his head back. He appraised his granddaughter as if examining an artifact covered with mysterious runes. When he found his voice, he couldn't keep the amazement out of it.

"Thanks, Sweetie, but what makes you say that?"

"I think people should do what makes them happy. They shouldn't be forced to do things that make everyone miserable."

"I agree," Walt said.

He put his arm around Loreen, who was now walking at his side, and they crossed the lawn in silence. But Walt heard his granddaughter's last words echo in his head, and suddenly he felt as if he was supposed to be someone else.

*　*　*

"Something's wrong with Loreen," Walt told Beverly as they sat down to dinner that night.

"Something's wrong with Loreen's mother," Beverly said.

"She sure isn't taking this well, is she?"

"No. But she's not making it easy for us, either."

"How are you going to deal with that vacation Bible school thing?"

"I'm making Carla deal with it, but I have to hand it to her: bringing over that Mathers girl was a stroke of genius. I almost didn't know what to do. That poor Judy Perkins didn't know what was going on. And that sweet little Tina kept asking if she was going to get to go to Bible school."

"I don't understand it."

Walt looked up from his chicken casserole and arched his eyebrows at his wife. Beverly shrugged her shoulders.

"At first I thought she just didn't want us to leave. Now I'm not so sure."

"Well, she's certainly letting us know she wants us here for some reason."

9

"But you know how she is, Walt. If everything's not in a certain order it drives her crazy. And when it is in a certain order it's usually because she's put it in that order, and that drives everyone else crazy!"

"No argument there."

"You've wanted this for so long. We've both wanted this for so long."

"I haven't known any other place," Walt said, staring down at his food and shaking his head. "I haven't been anywhere except here. At least you got to move around when you were young, even if they were mainly army bases. I was born 10 miles from here, and I've spent my entire life in Ordinary, waiting for a chance to see the ocean, the mountains, the canyons. I'm on a short stretch of road now, Bev. We both are."

"I know, darling. This should be your time. Our time."

Beverly poked the last bit of food on her plate then put down her fork. She finished the last gulp of tea and rattled the ice cubes in her glass like speeding up time.

"Maybe we should have just left in the middle of the night. It would have been a lot less stressful all the way around," she said.

Beverly reached across the table. Walt's fingertips found hers, curving back against them until they felt like they were hanging onto the edge of something.

*　*　*

Roger stood near the railing of The Whipper Snapper and wiped the sticky residue of cotton candy from his hands with a thin napkin. The mechanical whir of the amusement rides on the Sherman-Scott Circus midway intermingled with screams and shouts, and a variety of blinking lights punctuated the scenery. The late afternoon heat coaxed a few beads of sweat from his forehead as the air offered his nostrils the promise of popcorn and grilled hamburgers.

"What's going on, Sis?" Roger said.

Roger thought Carla looked distracted as she fidgeted with a sweaty plastic cup of Coke. She furrowed her brows and tilted her head to one side.

"What do you mean?"

"Come on, Carla. You're a bad liar."

The puzzled expression fell from Carla's face like raindrops trickling down a windowpane. She seemed to deliberate her response for a moment. Then she turned and scanned the crowd near the ticket booth.

"Where are the kids?"

"They're near the front of the line. Jason and Elaine are with Mom and Dad at the clown show in the main tent. We have plenty of time to talk."

Carla was silent. She did not look at her brother when she spoke.

"It's nothing."

"Something's going on, and I don't just mean tonight," Roger blurted out. He was surprised at his bluntness, and his throat felt dry. "I don't think you're fooling the rest of the family, either."

Roger searched her face. A thought struck him as he waited for his sister to reply.

"By the way, where's Tom?" Roger stepped closer to Carla as he asked the

10

question.

He wasn't ready for her response. She dropped her head and sighed a ragged breath. Even though she tried to turn and let her hair dangle in her face, Roger could see she had started to cry.

"Hey, Sis, I'm sorry. I didn't mean to push—"

"Everyone's leaving. Everyone's leaving me."

"What?"

Roger put his arm around her. He could feel her body shudder.

"First Tom. Now Mom and Dad. They're all going to leave me. Why is everybody leaving me?"

Carla's voice cracked between sobs. All the sounds and lights faded in Roger's ears, and all he heard and saw was his sister's distress.

"Oh, Sis, I'm sorry. I didn't know you and Tom were having trouble."

"I can't go through this alone," Carla whimpered. "Mom and Dad are supposed to be there. They've always been there. That has been the one thing I could count on. They're always supposed to be there."

Roger started to speak, wanted to offer consolation but could find only emptiness. This was not how it worked, and now he realized it with the clarity of a daydream. She shot a glance at him and then looked away and swiped at her tears.

When she spoke, her voice wavered. But she seemed to have read his thoughts.

"I'm supposed to be … I'm the big sister. I couldn't go to you with my problems. I'm the oldest; I'm supposed to do everything right."

"You know that's not true. Nobody expects that."

"I'm tired, Roger. I'm so tired."

"Give yourself a break, Sis."

As Roger hugged his sister he became aware of children's voices shouting. He and Carla followed the voice to an enclosed metal bucket that swung Rachel and Loreen in wild angles, near as an arm's length, then against a fading horizon.

Carla finished wiping her tears and waved. Roger waved, too, but mostly he was aware that his sister looked different, like a little lost girl.

* * *

Beverly took a deep breath and collapsed on one of the dining room chairs, the only furniture besides their bed that was left in the house. Walt ambled to the sliding glass door that looked out onto the backyard.

"I don't remember circuses smelling that bad when I was a kid," Beverly said, untying her sneakers.

"I think kids forget that part pretty quickly," Walt said. He barely moved.

Beverly stopped what she was doing and looked up at her husband. She studied Walt before she spoke.

"Is something wrong, Dear?"

"Roger told me something tonight. And it explains a lot."

"What is it? Is it something bad? Tell me, Walt."

Walt looked over his shoulder at his wife. He seemed to study her face.

"It's something that might change our plans. I've got an idea, but it'll be up

11

to you."

* * *

Roger turned in circles, letting his eyes sweep over the bare room. The Friday afternoon sunlight poured in through the windows making everything look open and new. Walt leaned against the doorframe.

"This room holds a lot of memories," Roger said. He dug his hands in his pockets and faced his father. "I got sent here so often for being bad, I almost forgot the rest of the house existed."

Walt chuckled and walked over to his son. He put his hand on Roger's shoulder.

"You're taking this much better than your sister. Last I heard, Carla was still trying to figure out why your mother and I are doing so much packing."

"Wait till she sees her room," Roger said.

"She didn't spend nearly as much time in her room for being bad as you did. She was old when she was still a girl."

Walt patted Roger on the back, then pulled his son to him and hugged him with one arm. Roger draped an arm around his shoulder and hugged him back.

"I'm worried about her," Roger said. They walked out of the room.

"I am, too," Walt said. "But we can't solve her problems for her. We can only offer advice, and we can't even do that if she won't ask for it. We'll always be there for her, but she can't control everything in her life."

"I know, Dad. She's never been good at asking for help though."

"She'll be fine. She just needs to get her bearings. Everything will be fine. You'll see."

* * *

Carla stood in the shade of her parents's porch and stared at Wilma Crowe, searching her face. Carla folded her arms.

"Excuse me for being so blunt, Mrs. Crowe, but what is going on? Mom and Dad aren't supposed to be leaving for another week. Then they call me Saturday night and tell me I have to meet them here Monday morning, and they're not even here. I demand to know what's going on."

Mrs. Crowe seemed to struggle to smile. She straightened her red blazer and adjusted the silver pin on her lapel that proclaimed her title as "Your Real Realtor."

"Let's wait for Roger," Mrs. Crowe said, turning away from Carla. "Nice day for a Monday morning, isn't it? Not a cloud in the sky."

"I don't understand why we can't just go in and wait for Roger inside," Carla said.

"I know, Honey. But I was given explicit instructions, and—" Mrs. Crowe raised her head, looking over Carla's shoulder. "Here's Roger now."

Roger parked his car behind Carla's and took three long strides toward the house. Taking two steps at a time, he bounded to the porch.

"Where's Mom and Dad?" he said.

Mrs. Crowe unlocked the front door without responding. Once inside, she walked over to the hall closet and opened the door, bending down to pick something up. When she emerged, she carried a basketball under one arm

12

"This is for Jason and Rachel," Mrs. Crowe said, handing the ball over to Roger.

Roger accepted the basketball without saying a word. His mouth had fallen open and seemed to have stopped working. Carla's expression mirrored her brother's, and neither of them moved.

Mrs. Crowe then reached into her blazer pocket and produced a set of keys on a key ring. She thrust them at Carla, who accepted them as if her reactions were now on automatic pilot.

"Those are the keys to your parents's van," Mrs. Crowe said. "They have arranged for you and your church to have full use of it this summer, including insurance coverage."

Carla turned to look at Roger. Roger shrugged his shoulders.

"What's going on?" Carla's voice barely broke above a whisper. She clutched the keys and pressed her fist to her chest.

But Mrs. Crowe had walked across the room and ducked into the kitchen. When she returned, she held out an envelope to Carla.

"They wanted me to give this to the two of you," Mrs. Crowe said. "I'll be outside on the porch if you still have any questions after you read it."

Carla stared after Mrs. Crowe. The envelope in her hand fluttered slightly.

"Roger?"

"Go ahead, Carla. Open it."

Carla did as she was told, her eyes and mouth wide. When she pulled the folded piece of paper out, Roger crowded closer to her to read it, letting the basketball drop to the uncarpeted floor. The hollow pinging filled the house.

As they read the note Carla put her hand to her throat. She fell back against the wall, slid down its length and sat down on the floor. Roger began to laugh. At first, only a few nervous giggles emerged from his lips. Then Roger's laughter came out full force, echoing in the empty room.

"This can't be real," Carla mumbled.

Still fending off the last of his laughing spell, Roger dropped down beside his sister. His eyes were wet.

"Do you mean to tell me ..." Carla said. She seemed to be incapable of finishing a sentence now.

"Yes," Roger replied, taking the note from her hand.

"Our parents ..."

"Yep."

"Our parents ran away and joined the circus?"

"Looks that way."

Carla exhaled a breath as if someone had just punched her in the stomach. Roger put an arm around her.

"I don't believe this," she said.

"I don't either, Sis, but it's kind of funny, don't you think?"

"Roger, how can you say that? What am I going to tell Loreen? What are you going to tell Jason and Rachel? 'Sorry, kids, you can't see your grandparents off on their trip; Grandpa is walking a high wire in tights, and Grandma is getting shot out of a cannon?'"

"Take it easy, Sis," Roger said, giggles spilling out between words. "I saw a Help Wanted sign at the circus that night we went. It was for the ticket booths. I'm sure that's what they're going to be doing. Last night was the last night the circus was in town; they must have left then."

Carla shook her head. Her shoulders sagged, and her back fell against the wall. She put her hand over her eyes and bowed her head.

"I drove them away," Carla said, her voice cracking.

Roger pulled his sister toward him, resting his chin on the top of her head.

"No, Sweetie, you didn't. They just had to do this, one way or another."

"I hate this, all of this."

"I know, Sis."

Carla went limp in her brother's arms. Her body shuddered with her sobbing, but she covered her mouth with her hands, trying to contain the sound. Roger patted her shoulder.

"Let it out, Sis. It's okay," Roger said. "A wise man told me he knew you would be fine, that you just needed to get your bearings. And that man has never lied to me."

For a few minutes, they sat there, curled up together. Roger let his eyes drift around the room. He saw two kids playing marbles on that same floor. He saw blankets draped between the sofa and chair, two young faces peering out at a monster movie on a television screen.

Then he felt Carla's body shaking more and more violently. He patted her arm, but Carla pulled away from him. And now Roger could hear his sister's laughter rising up her throat, like a long-imprisoned emotion.

"They ran away and joined the circus," she said, her voice booming. "Our crazy parents ran away and joined the circus."

Roger began laughing, too. He tried to stand while offering Carla a hand to pull her up. They both fell laughing onto the floor.

Carla's eyes were wet now. She reached over and hugged her brother, one of her hands still clutching the keys.

When they finally managed to stand, several minutes later, they were still laughing. Roger scooped up the basketball and cradled it in his left arm. They had tears in their eyes, and each of them knew it wasn't all from laughter.

Everything looked different. As they walked through the house, room-by-room, arm-in-arm, neither of them spoke a word. They stood in the backyard for what seemed like the entire morning.

They talked briefly with Mrs. Crowe when they stepped out onto the front porch. When the reached the driveway, they hugged again, and each of them turned to take a last look at the house.

Roger gazed up at the sky. Clouds had crept in sometime during the morning.

"Looks like rain," he said to Carla.

"Yeah," she said. "But we can't control the weather."

FALLING TOWARD GRACE

I.

She likes to wake me by leaning over me and talking. I've told her many times this is dangerous, and when I sit up with a start, reflexively balling a fist, I can swear I see a suppressed smirk beneath her look of surprise.

Then she apologizes and says she forgets. And breakfast is ready. Would I like some? I'm still almost embarrassed by my earlier reaction. But I think she wants something over me, because, awake, I give her nothing.

When I forgive her, I'm still disoriented. And it's like she's doing an end zone dance when she kisses my forehead and leaves me, my heart still racing, in a tangle of sheets.

II.

We knew each other a year before we became what other people call serious. I think the problem was we were always serious, but no one saw that.

Some of her friends warned her about me. I did, too.

Some of my friends warned me about me. I did, too.

But despite it all, or because of it all, we made the nights surrender to us. We stole the university campus for ourselves, sometimes until sunrise. And we grinned knowingly at everyone who said we were too different from each other to ever work out.

It was true on almost every level, to be honest.

I'm a dark-haired, coffee-eyed, permanently tanned suburbanite. Donna is a golden-haired, blue-eyed, fair-skinned country girl. When we met, I was talkative, jaded and openly looking for trouble. She was quiet, naive and secretly looking for trouble.

In that first year, we drifted between friendship and dating. And, looking back, I think it was best that way.

You see, she had had problems with guys before, and, in some way, I had known this from the moment I saw her. Not the specifics or anything. Just that something had happened to her, and it was like a shadow creeping over her soul.

I think that's why she fell in love with me to begin with: I saw in her immediately what others who had known her for years hadn't ever seen. Eventually I confronted her about it.

III.

It happened shortly after we met.

We had gone to a keg party at a friend's apartment, where I drank a lot and she watched a lot. Afterward, she had driven us back to campus. We were

15

just friends then.

Though she had parked the car near a lamppost, the angle was such that no light landed on her. And when I saw her in the shadows, I knew.

I knew my initial instincts had been right, because there is no need for the face to be cautious in the dark. And hers, which usually had the sweetness of someone who has no other defense, momentarily appeared empty, as if her life had drained away.

"You're not as happy as everyone thinks you are."
I said it just like that.

"What are you talking about?"
She sounded more like she was curious to know how I could tell rather than actually not knowing what I meant. So I told her.
I told her I thought she was still hurting badly from something in her past, that she was only happy on the outside because that's what everybody expected of her. I even had the nerve to tell her she was angry and scared about something but wouldn't confront it.

By the time I was done, she was sobbing softly into her hands. I began to regret saying anything, because nothing wounds me more than honest tears. Then, suddenly, she looked up at me and asked if I was the devil.

As much as I felt like I was at that point, I told her I wasn't. I told her I didn't understand why she asked me that question, and she told me she had learned in church that only two people can really know another person: God and the devil.

"And I know you're not God," she said.
She was right about that.
In a way.

IV.

The year after we met, I graduated with a degree in computer science. She was a year behind me. I moved to a town 50 miles away from campus and took on an entry-level position as a computer programmer at a small computer services firm.

We had developed an intimate relationship by then, so weekends usually involved one or the other traveling 50 miles. Mostly, it was her.

That's not to say I didn't want to see her or didn't care about her. I just seemed to have fewer opportunities to leave town than she did. Or maybe I just made it that way.

Still, we became closer with each visit, until she graduated with degree in communications the following year. Then she moved in.

Originally, it was a matter of convenience. Later, it became a matter of need.

Mostly, it was her.

V.

We are nature. We are the cycles of insects, trees and seasons. We are birth, growth, transformation and death. We are rebirth.

When we see ourselves as nature we are equal with it, a part of a greater organism that exists without regard to individual components. We become transitory.

Nowhere is that more true for me than at Silver Spring Lake. When I go there, I feel as if I am the same as the white-tailed deer or the woodland box turtle, nothing more, nothing less.

I used to try--successfully, on occasion--to get Donna to go fishing with me. But she thinks it strange to spend so much time trying to catch something only to release it. She doesn't like to bait her hook, either.

No matter. I enjoy fishing, even if I'm alone. Sometimes I even prefer to fish alone.

In fact, I used to go to Silver Spring Lake solely for the fishing. And even that did not differentiate me from nature, because the instinct to catch, to conquer, to dominate is no less natural than the one to blend in, assimilate and adapt. But I don't just fish when I go to the lake these days. I question. I wonder. And I evaluate.

VI.

From the beginning, we made things clear to each other about our expectations in the relationship.

I had many. She had none.

I told her I could never marry, because I couldn't promise fidelity to anyone. She didn't expect marriage.

I told her I was selfish. She didn't care.

I told her I had no time for petty emotions like anger or jealousy. She understood.

I told her I loved children but didn't want any of my own. She was fine with that.

For three years we lived together, and in that time, we changed each other. I gave her the confidence she lacked in herself and helped her become more outgoing. She gave me a sense of dependence and made me feel protective. All in all, she got the better part of the deal. And when I realized I was becoming a part of something, I resorted to severe tactics to rebel: I tried to be who I had been before we changed.

Many nights I left the house to be alone. I would often detach myself emotionally. I provoked discussions about how we were at a point in the relationship where we were becoming detrimental to each other.

Maybe it was because I was afraid nothing good could come of it anymore. She had no more to gain from me, so I gave her no more. I had too much to gain from her, so I refused to take it.

On more than one occasion I lost my temper. Many of my possessions were hers as well. And I sometimes found myself thinking about marriage. When I told her how I felt, it often ended up with me yelling and her crying. Her tears angered me even more, and when she wanted me to hold her I stepped away, like I was stepping away from the edge of a cliff.

Invariably, she agreed with what I said when I told her I thought our relationship could benefit from change. But that's all. That was always all.

17

Nothing would change.

And, turning her back on her degree, she added nothing.

VII.

Lately I've been defying Silver Spring Lake. My journeys there have become more frequent, and, more often than not, I resist the inclination to see myself as a part of my surroundings.

Still, sometimes the environment persuades me back. And I allow my connection to nature again, at least for a little while.

Standing at the edge of a bank, amongst the oaks and maples, crisp leaves beneath my feet, a breeze tussling the humanness out of my hair, I begin to see my fate again. I am part of everything, and everything is nothing more than one thing. And I know it is this place telling me that.

This lake has a sense of life and death and everything in-between. All around me, nature prods me with the sound of falling walnuts and the scent of decaying wood, the splash of fish and fragrance of honeysuckle, confiding itself to me with the whisper of the swishing rush and the sigh of the bowing reed until I feel out of place to be there with the wrens fluttering in the brush and the squirrels scurrying along from tree to tree.

But something holds me there, despite my apprehensions, and I think about tears and how I can't allow the embrace.

And that separates me from nature again.

VIII.

Not everyone is looking for someone to spend the rest of their lives with. Not everyone wants to wake up every day beside someone other than themselves. And some people are best at maintaining only the solitary lifestyle they lead.

When I first told Donna this, she seemed to understand. But as we've continued our relationship I realize that I no longer have that solitary lifestyle.

We've grown into something that, so help me, has changed what I think I want, and it has given her—because of her traumatic past—what she never thought she could have.

And this is dangerous for both of us.

IX.

The last time I defied Silver Spring Lake, I baited my hooks with guilt and pride, and they both seemed to sink just fine when I cast them into the water. But they were still there when I reeled in my line, and I sat on a fallen tree on the lake's shore casting out my line while watching fish jump futilely out of the water near the center of the lake.

I use both live bait and lures. Usually the live bait is red worms or night crawlers, but sometimes I catch crickets or grasshoppers.

When I finished fishing the lake that last time, I walked the path that took me along the feeder stream. Up about half a mile, the tree-lined banks give way to open shores. I've had some luck fishing these areas because the stream is wide and deep.

That day I used grasshoppers for bait because the high brush was thick with them. But nothing was biting for almost an hour, and, in my restlessness, I put down my fishing rod and began tossing sticks into the water, watching them float slowly at first, then quicker as they moved away from shore, and even quicker as they neared a line of rocks and spilled over.

At one point, I noticed a grasshopper clinging to one of the sticks I picked up. Shaking the stick did not prompt it to jump off; it simply pulled itself closer to the stick.

Intrigued by this, I tossed the stick into the water and waited to see what the insect would do. Truth be told, I expected the creature to make a jump for it, since I had thrown the stick relatively close to the bank.

Surprisingly, the grasshopper hung on to the stick, completely motionless. Jump, I thought. Jump.

The stick drifted away from the bank, dipping slightly as it gained momentum. The creature remained frozen.

Why doesn't it jump? Surely, some instinct is telling it its life is threatened. Carelessly, the current carried the sheltering stick and its clinging passenger toward the line of rocks.

In reality, the chance for escaping unscathed had passed, and any effort the grasshopper made now would be a dangerous, desperate act that most likely would be fatal. I was angry then. I don't know why. Or perhaps I do. I growled under my breath, "Jump, damn it!"

But, inconsiderately, the waters took the two with it as it spilled over the rocks to an unknown fate. They were both goners. They might have found a better shore, or they might have been destroyed by their own nature. And, somehow, I felt strangely responsible for the creature. Strange because I had been killing creatures like it for the past hour.

This was different, though. And I knew it.

So, faced with an epiphany I could not escape, I sat down in the clearing near the tumbling stream on that late afternoon and hung my head, unsuccessfully fighting back tears I had caused myself.

X.

When it started it had something to do with how she couldn't see how things hadn't changed. Or maybe it was how she was comfortable with the way things were and didn't care that I wasn't.

And then the other things came up, the things that don't mean anything except to one person. And they were all my things, and I began to see it. We were adrift, and we had long passed the point where the bank was within reach. It was dangerous and desperate now.

I hadn't planned on spending the weekend like that, especially Saturday night. But those things are rarely planned.

So we stood there, in the kitchen, antagonizing one another because that is easiest. And the rush of blood in my chest was like the sound of glistening water tumbling over itself as it neared a line of rocks.

For all we had been through, I didn't want to believe she thought we'd

19

survive the journey down stream. I guess I really thought I wasn't worth the risk, except to myself, because, after all, we are all best at destroying when it comes to ourselves.

I was yelling, then, and she was crying.

"Yes, Ted, I thought things were better. I'm sorry," she blurted between choked sobbing. "I don't know what to do unless you tell me."

Jump, my mind shouted.

"I always tell you, and it never happens," I screamed. "And that's not even the point. We're both in this thing, and we both should make the decisions, but you never say anything. You just agree to everything and then forget about it. I don't know how we can stay together like that."

"I don't want to live apart, Ted. I'm sorry you're not happy. All I want is for you to be happy."

Her last words trailed off in anguished tears.

She was wounding me severely, and I felt anger surging from within.

Jump!

I said nothing but turned away from her.

I could hear her struggle for composure.

"I'll leave by the end of the week," she said in a shaky voice.

The rocks were in sight.

Jump!

I fought back my own emotions, but I felt responsible. And I knew what the possibilities were. I knew there were other unseen shores.

So I turned, and looking into each other's eyes was too much for either of us. And she burst into new tears as she told me she didn't want to leave, and fearfully, she reached for my embrace. And fearfully, I embraced her and clung to her shaking body, my own trembling with doubt and hope.

We were both goners.

ACT LIKE NO ONE'S WATCHING

Did you get it? Where is it?

Dude, don't pull it out! Man, that's probably what all your dates say. Sorry. That was cold. But this living room seems smaller than I remember. Everyone in here keeps staring at us; it's like they know we're up to something.

There are three or four people in the den. Tara is in the dining room with some of the family. She said the eulogy will be brief, and then we'll all go out to the back yard. She's going to spread the ashes at the base of the dogwood he planted.

It would have been easier if one of us smoked or even if Tara smoked.

What did you tell Dana? You didn't tell her why you needed the ashes, did you?

Oh, no. Really? None of them were home? I knew Jeff would be at work, but what about her aunt? That figures. Of course they wouldn't be there; it would have been way too easy. They're all smokers; we would have hit the mother lode.

So where did you get the ashes? Who?

Sean? Her neighbor at the end of street? Sean "The Stoner" Stonefield?

Aw, man, you don't mean these ashes are ...

Aw, Dude, this is sacrilegious. Well, it would be if I weren't an atheist. It's sacrilegious for you. Cigarette ashes would have been bad enough, but a week's worth of ashes from some stoner's ashtray? Man, that's just wrong.

Aw, man, I can't believe this. Aw, man. This is ... this is warped.

Wayne hated roaches; now, for all intents and purposes, he is one. Oh, crap, don't get me started, Troy. We don't need to be laughing at a memorial service. Get it under control.

Let's go to the hallway. You can pass me the ashes there.

Come on. I know. I'm nervous too, Dude. Keep a straight face. Everyone's looking at us.

*　*　*

Okay. Hand it over.

A baggie? You put it in a baggie?

Well, I don't know. An envelope or something. Something that would have been easier to pour from. All right, all right. Look, before we go in, let's have a plan.

You're going to have to distract everyone. I'll walk over to the table and stand in front of the urn. You tell whoever's in there I'll need a moment alone. We don't have much time; it's a quarter til two.

No, I'll do it. I'm the one who just had to look inside the urn and ended up dropping it. Then again, you were the one who had the bright idea to use that candle to get a better view of the inside of the urn and ended up torching my hair.

Damn. We were his best friends, and now look what we're doing. We're making his memorial service look like an episode of Beavis and Butthead.

I know it was an accident. But maybe Tara shouldn't have trusted us to set things up. We're not thinking straight. It feels like a bad dream. We were The Three Musketeers, man. The Three Musketeers. We'll never throw darts and drink beer at K.C.'s Tavern again. We'll never go jumping off Snake Head Point into our favorite swimming hole. Do you realize we've done that every summer for almost 20 years?

How does a 32-year-old man die of a heart attack anyway? Is that what we have to look forward to in three more years?

I know. I know. Our luck, we'll probably live to be crotchety old men. That just makes it harder to understand.

Tara said his boss at Walker-Winston told her he was the youngest VP of Marketing in the company's history. That's like a 45- or 50-year-old ad agency, too. I knew he was going to buy a house when he made VP last fall. He always wanted a house like this ...

Yeah. I'm all right.

Oh, no. Oh, no, no, no. Don't look. This is horrible, man. Don't look.

Aw, man, we're going to hell. Well, you're going to hell. I'm going to be reincarnated as a dung beetle.

Don't look. Yeah, that's the sound of the vacuum cleaner. Yes, the same one we used earlier. She's sucking up some honey roasted peanuts into Wayne's ashes.

Shut up! Quit laughing, man, they'll hear you.

No, Dude, this is not like Wayne's very own Last Supper. Man, that is so wrong that you said that. Our friend is swirling around in a Hoover because of our clumsy asses, and all you can do is make jokes. He's in there with dust bunnies!

I can't help it, man; it's your fault. Don't get me laughing. Oh, crap, we are so friggin' warped.

Yeah. You're right about that. Wayne would have thought this was funny.

Come on. Straighten up.

Ready? Deep breath.

* * *

You okay? Yeah, I'm all right. I mean it wasn't even really Wayne being sprinkled around that tree. It was just a damn ceremony. All these funerals are for the living anyway.

I hate to say it, but I'm glad to be out of that house. I started feeling like everyone was—

You okay to drive us back? No, that's fine. Give me your keys; I'll drive.

Didn't you feel like everyone was watching us? I know I was just being paranoid, but I swear it was as if Tara knew.

I can't believe you kept a straight face when she said their marriage was "a joint partnership." Did you catch what she said when she sprinkled the ashes, when she said Wayne was being lifted to a "higher place?" I almost lost it. I still can't believe what we've done—

Dude, where's the seat adjuster? You're a freakin' giant. Oh, okay, I got it.

Mind if we drive around a bit? I'm not ready to go home.

It's a nice day, considering. How about we go this way? Get away from the town.

Everything's so bright. The sun's like a huge spotlight on this place, on us, on everything we did today. Why does it have to be like that? Like things can't be real when it comes to ceremonies. Everyone always acts differently when they think they're being watched. It's so fake, so dishonest. I wish—

Yeah, I'm all right. It's just ... I don't know. It's like everyone got to say good-bye to Wayne except for us. At least they believe they were saying good-bye to him, and that's what counts. I don't know about you, but for me the ceremony didn't have any meaning, because I knew it wasn't really Wayne's ashes.

Aw, hell, man. What am I griping about? It was our own damn fault—

What? You gonna be sick? Sure, I'll pull over. Hang on.

You gonna be sick? You sure? Then why did you need me to pull over?

The trunk? Sure. Hold on; let me find the lever. Okay. There. I popped the trunk. Now what's going on?

No way! Tell me you're lying, Dude. We've been driving around with Wayne in the trunk of your car? Tell me you're lying.

Oh, crap, Dude, what were you thinking? You're serious? You've got the vacuum cleaner bag in the trunk? Wayne is in the trunk? How—

Where are you going? Hey—

Okay, okay. This is not really happening. Troy is not walking to the trunk of the car to remove the remains of our recently deceased friend, and he's not going to bring him up here to ride shotgun with—

Hey, welcome back, Troy. How's it going, Wayne? You're looking a little ashy—

Damn it, Troy, what are we doing driving around with a vacuum bag containing the cremated remains of our best friend? I don't believe this.

Just get in and close the door. I think we should keep moving.

Great. This is great. I'm sitting in a car beside Bag-O-Buddy here, cruising the countryside. Does any of this strike you as wrong?

How? How is this better? Better than what?

Okay. Okay. You're right: I wouldn't want him thrown out with tomorrow's trash and ending up at the city dump either.

Yeah. Okay. You're right. I said you were right, okay?

To be honest, the thought had crossed my mind earlier to do the same thing. But I figured we had screwed things up enough already.

No. No, I won't think less of you, buddy. Go ahead, man, let it out. It's okay. It's okay. He was our best friend.

I've got to pull over for a minute. My eyesight's a little blurry. Give me a minute.

No, I'm not ticked off at you anymore, man. Sorry I got mad.

Give me a minute.

* * *

Okay. Yeah, I'm okay to drive. I'm okay.

No, I'm not going that way. We're not going home.

Remember what I said earlier? About ceremonies?

Yeah, well you and I didn't really get one. And you and I are the living, Troy.

We are the living.

It's a perfect summer day. It's a great day for The Three Musketeers to make one last jump at Snake Head Point.

A FABLE OF FREEDOM

I.

Carlos Castillo was dreaming of piñatas again. Bright, colorful burros and bulls with fringes and streamers pointing down at the happy, laughing children dressed in ponchos and sandals. And sombreros. And clean, fat women selling vibrantly-colored flowers.

And when he dreamed of the things he knew, it was a dream of a church on a hill with a cross atop its steeple and its dark doors wide open. But even that was wrong, for the building was simple and had sharp lines, and it was surrounded by a city of adobe houses where people had smooth faces and did not look up. And the path to the church was not a steep, arduous climb over long, flaking stone steps but a clear, winding passage easily traversed by the pious villagers.

"Carlos!"

Mamacita's voice grew louder as she made her way down the breezeway toward his bedroom. He did not answer. He kept his eyes shut and searched the adobe walls.

"Andale, Carlos! You are late!"

Bullet holes. Now he could awake.

The outer screen door squeaked on its hinges. Mamacita tapped on the interior bedroom door, then swung it open, allowing the hot morning sun to spill in. Not warm. Not particularly pleasant.

And the breeze. In Cara Linda, it was as it was. Not the scent of ripe cactus tuna wafting in over a rainbow desert. Not the smell of mountain snow melting into fresh crystal streams that tumbled over slippery gray stones.

The breeze smelled like chicken manure and freshly slaughtered goat, of diesel smoke and drying urine. Carlos inhaled a long breath.

"I could die in this house on such a morning," he said.

"Hurry and get ready."

"I would be happy."

"You cannot be happy. That is not the law."

The law. The words echoed in his head.

The law. No resident within three blocks of Town Square was to patronize the shops and businesses in that district between 9 a.m. and 5 p.m. The law. Those who are chosen as town vendors are required to report for work in the square each day before 9 a.m. in full costume, with supplies provided by the town. The law. Visitors to Cara Linda are not permitted beyond the three block perimeter of the square. The law. The lie.

The wooden screen door slammed. Carlos heard his mother shuffling down the breezeway, making her way to the kitchen to fix breakfast.

Carlos forced himself out of bed, grabbing his bathrobe from a hook on the back of the door. He trudged down the breezeway in his sweat pants and

25

T-shirt on his way to the bathroom. As he passed the large open storage bins used to keep extra sacks of dry corn feed, he ran his hand along the rough surface of a burlap bag. The bins, protected from the elements by only a tin awning, smelled of dry earth.

The memory threatened to surface, but he fought it. He showered, then slipped on his robe and stepped out of the bathroom into the breezeway, turning to his immediate right and entering the den. He lifted a set of keys off a short nail on the wall near another door that adjoined the main room of the grocery store.

The store smelled unfamiliar and looked strange, diffused sunlight barely penetrating the opaque front window. Carlos booted up the computer, the sensation of being watched making him straighten his posture.

A framed newspaper clipping hung on the wall over his left shoulder. He could feel his father's tired eyes peer at him from the photo of the obituary, the tribute to a much-loved grocer whose death two years earlier was called an accident.

The computer beeped and hummed. Carlos reached for the silver scoop in the grain bin behind the counter. The memory overcame him. He could not stop it this time. Sounds of a struggle. Protests from his father. Screams from his mother. Officers in the grocery store. Dull shock of pain in the back of his head. Sudden darkness.

As a child, Carlos used to bury his hands in the deep, wooden corn bin, letting the gritty grain trickle away between his fingers. It felt like infinite abundance. But now that memory was forever fused with the image of finding his father dead just a split second before being hit on the back of the head with the butt of a pistol, the sound of his mother crying as he regained consciousness on the floor near the corn bin.. He pushed the scoop deep into the grain, the scratchy scrape a bittersweet sound to his ears.

Carlos returned to his room and walked over to his wardrobe. He disregarded his button down shirts and Dockers slacks and found the tattered tan pants and cream colored peasant shirt.

As he donned his costume, he glanced at the top of his dresser. A picture of his parents. Papacito looked tired, with little life left in his eyes. It seemed to Carlos Papacito looked comfortable.

At 35, Carlos shared a remarkable resemblance to the old man in the photo. Certainly he had his father's face: coffee brown eyes, salt and pepper mustache and thinning, yet still abundant, dark hair. Even their builds were similar: average height, lanky frame, wiry limbs.

But something was always different when he compared himself to his father. And Carlos was not sure what.

He finished dressing and strode to the kitchen.

A flour tortilla was warming on a back burner of the stove when Carlos entered the kitchen. Mamacita, a blue gingham dress hanging loosely on her, was setting simple white dishes on linen placemats on the solid oak table.

Carlos felt of the tortilla and checked its underside. It was warm, and its dark brown spots were like age and history. When he took the first bite it was small, like taking a communion wafer, and when he swallowed it he thought it was what pride must taste like.

"I cannot leave here today," Carlos said, weakly. He slouched in his chair at the table.

His mother had taken the empty plate before him and filled it with food from the stove top.

"They will beat you," she said, setting the plate in front of him.

"They have already."

Carlos thought of a beating that had occurred two years ago. Sixty-one-year-old Antonio Castillo. Dead on the floor of his own grocery store. Killed by town officers for selling five pounds of corn to a town resident before the last tourist bus left Cara Linda one afternoon. Ironic, Carlos thought, since Papacito had always respected the law, even the new ones.

Carlos began to eat, greedily, filling himself with reality. He grasped the blue granite cup that held coffee, and his fingers tried to memorize its surface.

"They will take the store, mi hijo. It was all your father had, all I have. They took your father. They already have you."

Even before the beginning, Mamacita had embraced both her religion and the law, certain both had a place. She prayed when her husband died, then managed the store the way the chief officer told her to. To the back storage room she relegated the garlic cloves, soap flakes, and other staples. In the front room she displayed postcards, straw sombreros, and cheap jewelry. To Mamacita, there were laws for both the soul and the body.

"I cannot keep doing this," Carlos said.

Darkness lingered in the kitchen. Yellow light fell on Carlos, but none touched the side of the kitchen in which Mamacita sat. Shadows settled around her tired, pleading eyes.

"I know it is not what you believe in, Carlos," Mamacita said. "But it is the law now. It is the law, and if you don't go they'll … It is the law, Carlos."

In the beginning, Carlos had clung harder to his faith in his religion, believing things would get better. When his father died Carlos prayed his death would have meaning. He prayed each night his own life would have meaning, too. But the town's new laws made Carlos lose his faith in man, and each day the laws went unchanged, his religion changed instead. It became weaker because he did. And now he had faith in neither.

Mamacita looked down at her plate, eating her breakfast slowly, mechanically. Carlos saw a comfortable fear in her eyes, and even though he was not sure why, he became frightened for both of them.

"I'm sorry, Mamacita. Of course I will go. You are most important in my life, my sweet mother. You are my day's beginning and end."

Carlos felt penitent as he spoke. And when his mother smiled, he felt momentarily absolved for his selfish thoughts.

II.

Small puffs of gray dust rose around his feet as Carlos plodded down the brick street with his burlap bag of supplies, another bag on his shoulder. He thought he could feel life escaping through doorways and windows like weak breaths of air.

The bakery on the corner of his block was alive with activity, but the breads in the display windows were simple rolls and tortillas. The real bread—the pan dulce—was not permitted to be displayed until after the tourists left. The chief officer had deemed the colorful sugar toppings "too exotic and therefore inappropriate." Carlos knew that meant tourists expected a much simpler people with less-imaginative bakers.

When he was two blocks away from the square, Carlos passed an old man who was leaning against a wall and throwing up. The old man's unshaven face was pressed against the textured clay, and the left hand with which he balanced himself was missing half of its middle finger.

"You are too close, Manuel. And you are too real. Don't let them see you; it will only be trouble for you."

The old man did not look up as he waved Carlos away, motioning the way one soldier might to another to signify a strategy in a silent mission.

Carlos stopped to regard him. His frame was gaunt, and his sunken eyes were dark. But they were not comfortable.

Every so often, maybe just whenever he was well enough, Manuel would try to make his way to the town square. His defiance had gotten him several days of imprisonment and many beatings, but he hardly seemed deterred. Town residents whispered about how and why he lost his finger, but no once could really remember whether or not it had always been like that, and no one would ask him.

And still Manuel persisted, though he never made it to the town square before invariably being picked up by a perimeter patrol officer. Only one town officer and the chief officer typically patrolled the square, but in the three surrounding blocks, town officers were everywhere.

"Manuel, you know what will happen if you keep doing this," Carlos told the old man. "Aren't you afraid?"

"I am more afraid of what will happen if I don't keep doing this," Manuel said.

Most residents dismissed Manuel as a drunken hermit, but Carlos respected and envied the old man.

"That is some burden you carry alone; I am sorry."

Carlos quickened his pace to the town square, feeling afraid and humbled at the same time. They were already there when he arrived.

Francisco with his insincere, elaborately carved knickknacks. Rosa with the false, painted flowers. And Serina with the good corn tortillas which she stuffed with unfamiliar mixtures of food.

"You are late. It is after nine o'clock, Carlos. You should have started already."

The short large man was expressionless. He spoke like he was ordering from a menu. Another man, somber like the real town, stood behind Ricardo Vasquez.

"I overslept."

"That is no excuse."

"It is the truth."

Carlos studied Ricardo's face. The uniformed man looked old for 29. Though Carlos was older, he felt younger, mostly like a child.

Sgt. Vasquez stared straight ahead, over Carlos, and Carlos could not see into his eyes. That bothered him.

"I had to get more supplies," Carlos said. His voice was dry.

"You must keep yourself stocked with supplies; we pay for them, so it is no expense to you. We will overlook your trespass of the law this once, but you must not be late again."

"I was lying. I overslept."

"You must not be late again," Sgt. Vasquez said, ignoring Carlos.

As he reiterated his warning, Sgt. Vasquez stepped backward and turned on his heels. The other town officer executed the same turn. They marched like practiced politicians, feigning casualness yet keenly aware of their importance.

"They could die and be happy," Carlos said.

When town officers had first seen the paintings that hung in his home shortly after the death of his father, Carlos had hoped their interest was only a passing distraction. A day later, the chief officer visited Carlos and his mother, and Carlos had confessed to having painted them. The chief officer informed Carlos he would be a town vendor, and Carlos agreed only because he feared for the safety of his mother.

Carlos shook his head and began unpacking his cloth bag. He pulled out a palette. Not his. Paints. Not his.

From the bag on his back he pulled out a short easel. Not his. Canvas. Not his.

After setting up, he seated himself on the simple wooden chair provided for him and scanned the square. Smiling food vendors. Cleanly swept brick pavement. A group of finely dressed synthesizer-enhanced mariachis.

Not his. Not his. Not his.

The tourists were already wandering into the show area, having disembarked from the long silver motor coaches that resembled spaceships. They snapped photos, using the vendors as backgrounds or shot videos of the busy marketplace. They beamed at the local crafts and cuisine that were as foreign to Carlos as he appeared to them.

Carlos scooted his chair closer to the easel, looking at the ground to make sure a leg did not catch on the edge of a stone.

He gasped.

They had not seen. They must have been partially covered by his bag when he stood with it at his feet. And the officers hadn't noticed.

He fought back a rationed laugh as he looked up from his brown topsiders.

"At least my feet are truthful," Carlos said.

III.

A young woman with short, dark hair and large, dark sunglasses was leaning over Francisco and his crafts. Carlos could hear her voice, smugly superior and coldly condescending.

When she walked over to Carlos, she drew her sunglasses away from her face to gawk at the paintings. She smiled faintly at the portrait of two old women plucking chickens in a bare kitchen with dirt floors. She cocked her head at the picture of a cobblestone street flanked by unimaginative stucco houses where a villager in ragged clothing and an oversized sombrero nodded in siesta under the noon sun.

"These are nice," she mumbled.

"Surely you know better," Carlos said.

Flinching, as if she had encountered a strange beast, the woman took half a step back.

"You speak English?"

"Apparently you do not know better."

"How much?" the woman asked, nodding at the painting of the sleeping villager. Then she repeated the question in Spanish, slowly, as if addressing a child. "Cuanto cuesta?"

"It is worthless," Carlos said. His body had become rigid, and he was strangely aware of the hardness of the wooden chair on which he sat.

"Ten dollars," the woman offered, folding her arms and leaning back.

"It is yours."

Thinking herself lucky, the woman quickly extracted some bills from her small purse and handed them to Carlos. She smiled indifferently at him as she claimed her prize.

"Kathy, smile," another woman called.

The other woman, a petite blonde, aimed a camcorder at her friend. Several bags from local shops hung off her shoulder. "Hold up the painting."

Kathy grinned for the video camera and raised the painting. She positioned herself beside Carlos.

Feeling the red burning his cheeks, Carlos turned to his easel. He tried to return to work, but he was violently aware of his surroundings.

"I like your little town," Kathy told Carlos. Then she caught herself. "Mi gusto su ciudad."

Kathy's words were accompanied by a sort of charade. She stretched out her arms and swiveled at her waist. Then she placed her right palm to her heart. Smiling, she turned to leave.

"You have not seen my town," Carlos said to the woman's back. "I am partly to blame for that."

It was nearly noon now, a time when the square was most unfamiliar to Carlos. A second assault of motor coaches had arrived an hour after the first, and now a third wave of foreigners were dispatched to violate the town.

Carlos had turned away from the scene, trying instead to concentrate on the nameless town of unknown people he was creating with his paints. But the square was filled with voices that were unwelcome, and he knew he was one of them.

"We are whores, you and I," he said, as his eyes swept over the square.

Several strangers admired his paintings, talking amongst themselves. Carlos did not pay attention.

He stood up to stretch his legs and looked down at his bare feet. He regretted having hidden reality in the burlap bag earlier, but after all, Ricardo would have noticed sooner or later. Then it wouldn't have been Carlos who would have suffered; it would have been his mother.

Carlos tossed down his paint brush and reached into the right pocket of his pants. He did not need to see them; he could feel the smooth, perfect shells and the sharpness of their tips.

For a moment he smelled the dust rising from a corn bin within a small, darkened general store. It mingled with the scents of perfumed soap flakes and hanging cloves of garlic. And his father was there, solemnly and contentedly waiting on customers, then flashes of him on the floor, sounds of a woman's sadness.

The memory swung like a pendulum, alternately soothing Carlos and angering him. He tried to remember the town the way it used to be, but the memories evaded him.

Cara Linda, as he knew it, would die before long unless Ricardo and his officers were exposed. And in some way Carlos knew it wouldn't have made any difference if he had left his shoes on.

An unfinished painting awaited him, and now he was invigorated with new motivation to complete the work. He absently found his paintbrush and began populating the back street market scene he had started, painting in people who hurried through the streets.

But the villagers of this town were not rushing from shop to shop, filling old burlap shopping bags with food and groceries. The half dozen people who scattered about the streets were moving away from an alley entrance where two town officers had just executed an old man while another officer watched.

The old man, who resembled so many people Carlos knew, was slumped in a pool of blood. The alley wall was riddled with bullet holes that resembled eyes, and each eye shed crimson rivulets of tears.

When he finished the painting, Carlos leaned back and appraised it. Around him, several strangers stood aghast.

"This is my town," Carlos muttered.

IV.

Ricardo closed the door behind him and took a seat behind his desk. To either side of him stood a town law officer, and behind each of them was a plastic plant that resembled foliage that was native to areas much further south.

Carlos stood facing Ricardo, trying to disregard the audaciousness of the décor. An Aztec calendar hung on the wall behind Ricardo. Clay pottery and turquoise jewelry rested on rough pine shelves.

Instinctively, Carlos reached into his pocket and withdrew a balled fist that held the small realness of three kernels of corn. No one else saw this.

"Your little stunt upset me," Ricardo said.

"Nothing could have represented this town any better than my last painting," Carlos said, raising his chin.

Ricardo gestured with each hand to his officers, and they moved to Carlos. The taller of the two officers pinned Carlos's arms to his sides. Carlos clenched his teeth just moments before the other officer struck a swift blow to his midsection.

"You will paint what we tell you to paint!"

Carlos could not hear what Ricardo was saying. The officer had knocked the wind out of him, and the room went dark for a moment. The blow had caused him to double over and fall forward, his knees dropping toward the ground. But he would not let them touch the tiled floor.

31

During the assault, Carlos lost his grip on the kernels, and they fell to the floor, almost lost within the colorful tiles. The shorter officer quickly gathered them, then held them out for Ricardo to see. The chief officer eyed the grain indifferently and waved them away. The shorter officer dropped them in a wicker waste basket beside the desk.

Gasping for air, Carlos broke from the taller officer's grasp and dove toward the waste basket. Ricardo shot out of his chair, his eyes wide and his pistol drawn. The officers grabbed Carlos before he could reach the waste basket. Though he was surprised at his need to reclaim the kernels, Carlos was more surprised at Ricardo's reaction.

Glaring at Carlos, Ricardo regained his composure and holstered his gun. Carlos stood up straight as the officers on either side of him held his arms.

"You will return from you 'lunch break' and paint what you are assigned to paint," Ricardo said. "And at the end of your work day you can explain to your mother what happened. I'm sure she is wondering at this very moment why my officers are locking up her store."

Carlos began to speak, to protest, but no sound would come from his mouth now. He could not feign surprise because he had known the risks all along.

"I will paint your town because I have no choice," Carlos said. "But one day it will be you who has no choice."

Holding his head up, Carlos turned his back on the chief officer and walked to the busy town square.

V.

Carlos felt miserable as he made his way home in the late afternoon sun. His back ached from sitting on the wooden chair all day, and the burdens he bore on his shoulders seemed heavier than usual. Carlos had remained barefoot when he left the square, because after his confrontation with Ricardo the town guards watched him very closely. And now his feet were sore and scratched, and his body felt tired.

"Move back!"

The voice startled Carlos. He had been lost in thought, looking down at the smoothness of the cobblestone street. Now he stopped to take in the scene before him.

Two town officers stood at the entrance of a narrow side street. They directed a small gathering of town residents to move along. Beyond the officers, EMTs rolled a stretcher to a waiting ambulance.

Red wetness seeped into the white sheet that covered the body. Even from where he stood, Carlos could see one of the lifeless arms hanging from beneath the sheet. It was the left arm, and its hand was missing half a middle finger.

"You got what you wanted, my friend—what I still want. I envy you that," Carlos mumbled. He felt alone and somehow saddled with more responsibility now.

When he had traveled three blocks he came to the store. The shutters were closed, and the bare doors were padlocked.

Carlos felt as if the wind had been knocked out of him for the second time

32

that day. He barely paused in front of the still, silent building for fear of seeing his father.

Stepping up to the adjoining home, Carlos reached for the door handle and depressed the thumb latch. The door was locked. He took a step back and looked at the living room window. The curtains were drawn.

The late afternoon sun splashed a deep red all over the streets, and Carlos knew that the beautiful glow of such a day normally would be welcomed into his home. He hurriedly found his keys and unlocked the door.

The living room was dark. He dropped his supplies and rushed through a pair of French doors into the den.

Carlos almost passed through the den before he realized his mother was there. It was only her gentle sobbing that made him aware of her presence. She sat in a chair near the door to the grocery, her left hand over her eyes, her right hand curled into a fist in her lap.

"Mamacita—"

As he knelt before his mother, Carlos realized he did not know what to say.

He glanced at the door to the grocery store. It was boarded up. Carlos thought the planks across the door frame looked like the lid of a pine box coffin.

"They have taken the store, Carlos," Mamacita said, weakly. "What can I do now? That is the last of it. There is no more."

The crimson light crossing from the breezeway door did not reach the hollowness of Mamacita's cheeks and eyes. And only half of her face was touched by the setting sun.

"I'm sorry, Mamacita. It is my fault. I defied them. I was so angry, Mamacita. I'm sorry."

"They have taken it for two weeks; they have taken it forever."

Mamacita turned her head toward the grocery store door and closed her eyes. She hung her head and crossed her hands on her lap.

He left her in silence. He walked through the breezeway to his bedroom, lifting his eyes to the open sky and the spongy white clouds that drifted unrestrained.

There was no scent of waiting food drifting from the kitchen like there always was at the end of his work day. And it wasn't that he was hungry. What frightened Carlos was his knowledge of what food it was that had been taken away from Mamacita.

That night Carlos went to bed with a head full of concerns and an empty stomach. When he slept, he dreamed of carefree villagers dancing in the streets, of quaint stores filled with decorative clay pottery and of pretty young women being serenaded in the moonlight from the streets outside their bedroom windows.

VI.

On the afternoon of the second day Carlos called a doctor. Because Ernesto Garcia was a friend of the family, the physician was able to arrange to stop by the house early in the evening.

Carlos explained how Mamacita had not left the chair for two days, eating nothing and drinking only a glass of water. Carlos felt ashamed that he had to leave Mamacita during the day, but he knew Ricardo would only make things worse if he failed to report to work.

"She will not last two more days like this," Dr. Garcia said, after examining his patient.

Carlos nodded in assent as the doctor made plans to have Mamacita transported to the hospital. Only when he hugged his mother in grief did he elicit any response from her, and even then Mamacita only lowered her eyes and began to cry.

In that moment, Carlos inexplicably became aware that her left hand was balled into a tight fist, and he did not realize this until the EMTs arrived and struggled with her to remove her from her chair. Then, just before they forced her weak body onto the gurney, Mamacita grabbed her son's hands and placed in them three tiny kernels of corn.

VII.

On the morning of the third day, Carlos awoke from more bad dreams crying. He had dreamed he saw his parents together, but their faces were different somehow, and then he saw the store, and the things on the shelves and behind the counter were strange foods and cheap, imported trinkets. And he did not recognize the people shopping at the store, and many villagers were behind the counter, as if for sale, but they did not look like anyone he knew.

Carlos had not gotten much rest. When he was asleep, he was plagued by nightmares, and when he was awake, he was vexed by reality.

By the time his alarm clock normally would be going off, he had already showered and dressed himself. Even though he had flipped on the lamp on his bedside, his bedroom was filled with shadows. His hands searched the top of his dresser for the tiny kernels of corn he had left there because he could not trust his eyes. He found two kernels and put them in his pants pocket.

Carlos saw the morning sun rising when he stepped into the kitchen, but it was a hotter, brighter sun than he had ever seen, and he knew it was not right.

After a breakfast of two buttered tortillas and a cup of coffee, Carlos called the hospital to check on his mother. The nurse in charge told him she was being fed intravenously but was not doing much better than when she was admitted.

"It is the same as father," Carlos thought sadly, harshly. "They are only using a different weapon."

As he gathered his supplies together in his room, Carlos became angry. He was angry with the town. He was angry with the town officers. But mostly he was angry with himself, because he realized everything was his fault. He had not completely fought nor had he entirely complied, and his non-commitment came with a price.

The thought crept into his mind. It was the same thought that had its origins the night before, when his head pounded with memories, guilt, and hatred. It was a thought that frightened Carlos because it was not like him; it was antagonistic and violent. But it was also a possibility, and that was what he was like now: a man desperately searching for a possibility.

Carlos opened the bottom drawer of his dresser and pushed aside several

34

pairs of socks. He picked up the sheathed knife that lay in the corner and pulled the blade out of the leather casement. The silver weapon gleamed brightly. He ran a trembling hand along the knife's edge, and its sharpness was evident. His hand shook as he put the knife and its sheath in the paint supply box.

Then Carlos searched his wardrobe for a light vest, but he could not find one long enough. When he finally found one that extended well below his waistline, it was one that had been his father's, one he had picked out of the back of his mother's closet.

At first Carlos was afraid to put on the vest, and he began to feel sad again. But when he looked at the photo on the dresser, he realized he could not look so much like his father anymore, and he smiled a faint, knowing smile.

VIII.

The morning air was brisk when Carlos stepped out into the street. His sandaled feet felt strange, almost comfortable, and the supplies he carried felt much more natural than usual. As he realized this, Carlos walked with a quicker stride down the silent street.

The town square looked frightened of the dawn sunlight. The buildings seemed to draw away from the curbs like children stepping away from strangers. Carlos could feel the comfort of night and darkness ebbing away into the violet sky.

No one else was there yet. He would be alone on the square for some time, and it was this opportunity that hastened him to set to work. For the next half hour his small, thin hands were busy splashing strokes of earth colors on a barren canvas. Twice, to reassure himself, he reached into his pocket. He found a single kernel of corn.

By the time the square began to come to life with the early vendors and town citizens, Carlos was oblivious to anything but his work. He skillfully painted the Cara Linda skyline, surrounding it in the foreground with a richly textured desert and in the background with a range of purple mountains. And, though the painting incorporated an impressive amount of shadowing and contrast, it was not so much a detailed rendering that it took his trained hands too long to complete.

Once or twice while he painted, Carlos stopped to pull out other pictures he had completed earlier in the week and had not yet sold. Visitors drifted by, appraising these works, but they invariably turned their interest to his work in progress.

The second bus of visitors had arrived some time before Carlos finished his painting. The crowd of strangers felt smothering, closing in around him. It was time to start, but he was not ready. He reached into his trouser pocket, but he could not find it. He knew everything had to come from him now. His heart had begun to race, and he could feel his temples become tight.

"What a beautiful portrait of your town."

Carlos turned to face the stranger who had spoken. It was a woman, probably in her late 50's, and she peered at the painting over the top of her bifocals. Half a dozen other strangers moved in to take a closer look.

"How much is it?" a male voice asked.

35

But Carlos was not paying attention. He was craning his neck in search of something in the square.

"Is it for sale?" another voice asked. And now a dozen strangers had gathered around the artist and his work.

Carlos spotted him. The town officer made his way purposefully toward the scene. About 50 yards away—intentionally unaware of any minor police matters—Ricardo socialized with some of the visiting strangers.

With a faint smile, Carlos once more turned his attention to his work. He replayed the questions in his head and began to respond.

"This portrait is not yet done," Carlos said, not particularly loud and to no particular person.

At that same instant, the crowd parted for a uniformed officer.

"Good morning, Thomas," Carlos said, smiling. "As you can see, I am in the process of painting a picture even Ricardo would covet."

"Buenos dias," Thomas said, in a corrective fashion. "That is a fine portrait you have painted."

The officer's stance relaxed a bit, but his hands mechanically swung around his sides and interlocked behind him. He looked conspicuous among the strangers and even among the town people, and Carlos thought it was because—like the other town officers—he could claim nothing else.

"I have a problem, Thomas," Carlos said. "I cannot finish the work without more supplies, more paint. I thought I had plenty, but …"

Carlos shrugged his shoulders in an expression of helplessness.

"I know Ricardo would wish me to finish this work so that these nice visitors might consider purchasing it. But you understand how Ricardo … well, insists that I not leave my place here."

As Carlos finished speaking, several of the strangers turned to Thomas, anticipating his response. The officer scowled at the implication, careful not to allow the visitors to see his displeasure.

"What is it you want?" Thomas asked. "You want me to request permission from Ricardo for you to leave?"

"Oh, no, Thomas," Carlos hastened to answer. "I could not put you in that position. But if you could bring me a fresh supply of paints from the town supply room, I'm sure Ricardo would approve. And I, of course, would be grateful."

The officer paused.

Carlos crossed his hands so as not to appear nervous. But he knew everything depended on what Thomas would say next, and he knew his courage might never be as strong again if this should fail.

Thomas straightened his posture then took two inconsiderate steps toward Carlos so that he stood only inches away from him. With a forced smile, he leaned down and spoke with fragile complicity.

"I will be back momentarily with your paints. And I am sure Ricardo will understand the predicament when I explain it to him afterward."

The officer turned with a snap and moved through the crowd. Carlos waited until Thomas had crossed the square, then he began at once, for he knew his time was limited. The crowd was still inching closer in uncomfortable familiarity.

"I am about to commit a crime," Carlos announced. "I am going to leave this job as town artist. That may seem ridiculous to you, but freedom does not exist in Cara Linda because of Chief Officer Ricardo Vasquez and his men. They have already taken my father's life, my mother's health and our property. They have, in fact, taken my life by keeping me here—or rather by intimidating me to believe I must stay here. But now I have nothing left to lose."

The crowd murmured dubiously.

"Is this a performance of some sort?" one young man asked.

"Before I leave, I must complete this portrait with the one element that makes the town what it is."

It was then the strangers saw Carlos held a knife in his right hand. Many onlookers gasped, and some turned and hurried away from the scene. But most of the spectators simply stepped back and waited, transfixed by curiosity.

Holding up his left hand, Carlos ran the blade across the palm until red life streamed down the rough flesh and met near the wrist, where it formed into drops and fell. As he balled his left hand into a fist, he tossed the stained knife into his painter's box with his other hand. Then he bent down and deftly closed the box, hooking a small padlock into the latch.

Carlos moved his cut hand over the painting so the blood dripped on the Cara Linda sky, using the paint spatula to form the red into clouds. He allowed many droplets to run down into the town.

By now the crowd had distanced themselves from the painter. Their voices nearly roared in a deep cacophony of confusion as Carlos completed the last few strokes. No one noticed him move his right hand under his vest.

Surely it would happen now. With Thomas gone and all the other officers on perimeter duty, he would have to handle it himself. He would come, and it would be over.

Carlos felt weak. He felt elated. And he felt ethereal.

"What is going on here?"

Ricardo's voice boomed over the rumblings of the crowd. His face was contorted into a visage of fury.

"The truth is what's going on here, Ricardo. I cannot give any more to this town; that is the last of it. Whatever more you need you will have to take against my will."

"Carlos, come with me."

"I will not. And I have something to give you."

As he stepped toward the chief officer, Carlos flipped back one side of his vest to reveal a knife sheath from which protruded a wooden hilt. Ricardo frantically motioned with his left hand for the crowd to move away. With his right hand Ricardo pulled out his pistol. Screams bounced off the buildings and filled the air. Most of the visitors close to the scene dropped to the ground.

"I've wanted to do this for a long time," Carlos said, lunging toward Ricardo as his hand tugged at the wooden hilt in the knife sheath. "This is for you."

A blast, then another, pierced the turmoil. Carlos stumbled backward at the force of the impact. His left shoulder stung, and his abdomen felt hot with wetness.

He struggled with all his effort to keep conscious.

"How ... does it feel to be forced ... forced to choose?"

Carlos stared coldly at Ricardo, then glanced triumphantly at his own out-stretched hand. Ricardo instinctively followed his gaze.

Moments before Carlos collapsed in a motionless heap before him, Ricardo caught sight of the weapon the painter was wielding. He grumbled a soft curse as the blood-stained spatula fell on the bricked square.

IX.

"Not so fast, my friend," the blurry figure said.

Carlos felt his head throb, and he realized he had tried to sit up. Although he could not quite focus his eyes, the voice was familiar.

In a few seconds he was aware of the sounds of machines and the antiseptic smell of stainless steel. And there was something else, something that smelled sweet. He began to speak, but his throat hurt from dryness.

"Just lie back and take it easy, Carlos," Dr. Garcia said. "Your doctor tells me you are very lucky. The bullet in your shoulder did very little damage, and the one in your torso only nicked a rib."

Carlos could feel the dull pain now. He let himself settle back into the hospital bed.

"You lost a lot of blood, Carlos," Dr. Garcia continued. "Not only from the gunshot wounds, but from that crazy stunt you pulled on your hand. Your doctor tells me you'll be here for a few days. I came to see how you were doing."

The doctor paused. He studied Carlos for some time. Then he grinned.

"I guess you'll be happy to know it worked," he said. "The governor has ordered a full investigation on Ricardo and his officers, and they have all been suspended until the investigation is complete. We have a new temporary police force, and they operate the town the way it used to be before Ricardo."

Carlos inhaled the sweet scent that lingered in the air. He shifted his eyes to his immediate left, to look at the table beside his bed. Flowers blossomed from several vases of various sizes.

"It seems several tourists photographed the incident, and a couple of them even videotaped the whole thing. That's mostly what started the investigation, but then I sense you planned that."

Carlos managed a smile. He closed his eyes for a moment, and when he opened them his vision was once again blurry.

The whole time Dr. Garcia spoke, Carlos studied his surroundings. He could see various pieces of modern medical equipment, hear the hum of the fluorescent lights overhead, feel the stiff roughness of the bed linens.

"Most importantly, Carlos, you're mother is doing well. As soon as she heard the close order on the store was lifted, she began to improve. She is still worried about you, of course. But I'm sure you'll get to see her soon, after she is well enough to be discharged. That may be as soon as tomorrow."

Dr. Garcia leaned forward in the chair next to the bed. He could see the heaviness in Carlos's eyes, yet they seemed to gleam brightly in their centers, like golden specks of grain in the sunlight.

With a soft sigh, Carlos closed his eyes again. Dr. Garcia reached over and touched his friend's arm, as if checking a burner on a stove.

"Do you understand, Carlos? It is over."

But Carlos was dreaming now. He was dreaming of old hobbled men with fingers missing and gray stubble on their faces. He was dreaming of decorative sweet breads with pink and white sugar toppings. And he dreamed of dusty corn bins in grocery stores where the scent of powdered detergents mingled with the sharp odor of hanging garlic.

And as he dreamed, Carlos smiled.

A STRANGER'S PLACE

It was a cool night. A nice night, the old man said to himself. On a night like this there was rebirth. There was a rebirth of the wonder the old man had felt as a youngster when he looked upon the cloudless, starry sky. There were so many of those nights. And there was a rebirth in the ocean before him, the ocean that shifted endlessly and held so many secrets. The dark waters had been inviting to him as a child, and now that invitation was renewed.

The old man sighed.

"Vamos, papacito," the young man said. He was the old man's grandson, and he was twenty.

"No," the old man said. He had heard Miguel make his way down the wharf. He was not surprised. "No. You sit with me."

The darkness at the end of the wharf concealed the two figures. The old man felt safe there. He could look up and down the beach and not be seen himself. He could admire the sky and the slightly discordant sound of the waves rolling on the shore as they made a hollow echo under the wharf.

The ocean breeze was pleasant, too. It was the same breeze that touched the shores of Mexico before it swept across Corpus Christi Bay. It carried the salty smell of the water along with it, but the old man did not mind. He was used to it, and he even liked it. It did not destroy the peacefulness he felt as he sat at the end of the abandoned wharf.

No one else was there now. The wharf was long out of use. Even the fishermen seldom used it because years ago a storm had taken half of it away, and now it was short, and there were no floodlights.

For a while, the old man felt that he owned this place. This place was his as a boy. This place always welcomed him and made him feel that he belonged.

"Mama and Papa were worried. They were looking for you."

"Sit with me," the old man said again.

Miguel slowly took a place beside the old man.

"Now it is complete."

"I knew you would be here," Miguel said. "I told them, and they didn't believe me."

The old man looked at Miguel.

Miguel could see he was thinking.

"Remember how I used to bring you here? You were just a boy then. A little boy. You liked feeding the seagulls just as much as I did when I was a boy. Recuerdas?"

"Yes, papacito," Miguel said. He had always called the old man "papacito." It was a term his father used, and Miguel had picked it up because he knew it was a nice word.

"Now look at you; you are watching over me now."

The old man looked away. His eyes were old, but in them, there was life.

"Because I don't want to see them put you away."

"You have compassion to replace that which your father lacks."

"He loves you, papacito. He was just so worried. The doctors said you need professional care."

The old man laughed a short, bitter laugh.

"I need no help in dying."

There was a silence for a minute. But it was only silence between the old man and his grandson. The ocean was still roaring. Along the beach, there were now three boys playing near the water. Their laughter was carried the distance by the ocean wind and died before the sound was completely comprehended.

The old man began gazing at the sky. Immediately, his grandson followed his stare. The sky was full of light. Sometimes the lights got brighter before they faded, but they were always there. From out of nowhere, a shooting star appeared. Its instantaneous flash of light was followed by a quick demise and sudden darkness. Both the old man and his grandson had seen it.

"It is like life," the old man said.

Miguel did not respond.

"I am just an old fool," the old man explained.

There was the silence again. The old man turned his gaze upon the water. The waves were becoming choppy and short. Miguel shifted slightly.

"Let's go, papacito."

"No. I am not sure you understand. Besides, I am too weak now."

"Why did you come here if you were so weak? You shouldn't be out."

"I cannot live among strangers," the old man said.

"You're not going to live with strangers. Papa said you won't have to go to a home if I take care of you."

"I am not talking of a home. I am a stranger among my family."

"No, papacito, you're not."

"Not with you, chiquito. But with your father and his wife. They no longer like to think about me. They cannot accept an old man now."

"They try, papacito. They really try."

"I cannot live among strangers," the old man said again. "And I will not die among them."

The old man's voice was soft now. Miguel looked at the old man for a long time.

"I'm sorry," Miguel said.

"It is not you."

"I know, but I'm still sorry."

"We are all strangers, Miguel. But every stranger has his place. This is mine."

"And where is mine?"

"Right now it is here."

Miguel was still staring at his grandfather. The old man was beginning to look tired now. He had left the house without much difficulty earlier that afternoon while Miguel was out. He was not missed until Miguel returned, and it was late in the evening now.

Miguel could not help but notice the tranquility in the old man's face. It was not a look of resignation or even a look of forced composure. It was more a look of quiet satisfaction. Miguel smiled. After a few minutes, he put his arm around the old man's shoulder.

"I love you, papacito," Miguel said.

"I know, chiquito," the old man whispered. "And you will understand me soon. You are the only one who will."

The old man's voice trailed off. It was a hoarse, sickly voice, and Miguel did not like it. It did not sound like his grandfather.

Miguel watched his grandfather's eyes slowly shut. The old man's body became limp in Miguel's arms. Miguel did not move. Instead, he gazed at the ocean. The waves glistened in the moonlight, and now and then Miguel could see a fish jump to the surface. There was a small jellyfish directly below him that had been drifting in front of him through the latter half of the night. Miguel did not notice it until now. He watched it move. It was a shiny, crystal animal with a luminous, opaque body, and Miguel did not realize it before, but it was beautiful.

It was getting cold now. The ocean breeze was slightly stronger. But Miguel did not mind. He liked the ocean breeze. He liked the ocean. He liked looking up at the sky on nights that were clear. He searched the heavens and looked at each star.

He did not know how long he sat there. His legs were getting stiff, though, and he was beginning to feel sleepy. Still, he was not tired of being there. He wanted to stay there all night. There would be a beautiful sunrise, and the seagulls would begin to gather in large groups, making a sound that the old man used to call the "song of the ocean." He looked around him again. He gazed at the ocean, the beach and the skyline. He was still fascinated with the place. He had been there for a while. He did not know how long, but he would have to leave soon. He stayed longer, though.

But he knew his parents would not worry now that he had gone looking for the old man. They trusted him even if they did not know why. The old man was Miguel's responsibility. He had brought the old man back from his wanderings many other times, although this was not a wandering.

Finally, Miguel looked at the old man again. His face still looked tranquil.

"I understand, papacito," Miguel whispered. "The ocean is the only place you could ever belong. It was the only place where you weren't a stranger. And I'm not a stranger to you or it, either. And my being here did make it complete."

Miguel looked away from the old man. He scanned the light brown beach. It was dotted with thousands of bone-white seashells. But even from where he sat, Miguel could see the decomposing carcasses of several sea animals. He began to gaze at the sky again. In the distance, he heard the sound of several seagulls that had alighted on a faraway reef.

"And this place is beautiful, and the sky is nice when it is full of stars. And that shooting star is like life—just like you said. It doesn't last long enough. And everyone is a stranger, and you are lucky to find someone who is not a complete stranger. And you knew all along that I would find you here. And you knew all along that you were going to die here. You even knew that I would stay here after you died and try to understand everything you said. You knew I would. I do understand now, papacito. I do."

The waves were loud upon the shore. They made a sort of echo under the wharf that Miguel liked to listen to. It was a sound that was familiar to him.

"I understand, papacito," Miguel said aloud. "But I almost wish I didn't."

A SCENT LIKE DAPHNE

She calls him "Daddy" as he dresses, and this, for him, is the worst kind of truth she has ever uttered. The word is a stray bullet, piercing his starched white shirt and red silk tie, the armor he carries like a shell. His now mute body—a swimmer's build out of water—squirms under his other skin.

"Don't call me that," he tells her, the taste of sex and regret lolling around in his mouth, the aftertaste of her skin.

When he turns to look at her, he realizes he towers over everything, floating above what is real and what is manufactured. He can't look her in the eye for fear she will see the shape of his soul, but he suspects she has plied her own shapes in him, her own elastic strands of complacency and control.

He finds his jacket on a scarred Salvation Army Thrift Store chair and walks toward the bedroom door. With too much ease, he thinks to reach into the breast pocket of his jacket where his sunglasses are. He doesn't feel the absurdity of putting them on in the dusky room.

The whole apartment is cluttered with her clothes, a misleading trail of lacey bras and panties, Lakewood University jerseys and mismatched socks. They writhe and curl on the floor, on furniture, on doorknobs.

They hang out of a dresser that looks like it came from the children's section of a furniture store. A moth-eaten bedspread, thin enough to let some of the daylight in, cascades over the curtain rods. Jasmine tinges the air in wisps like whispered promises.

"Whatever," she says, sitting up in bed. "Just don't count it against me, professor."

She drops her chin and feigns a pout, letting her hair dangle over her breasts, vines sheltering a garden arch. When she grins, she shows all her teeth. She reaches for her cigarettes and lighter on the bedside table, and he catches a glimpse of the butterfly tattoo on her shoulder, as small and fleeting as a birthmark. The sheets covering her legs form ridges where shadows can hide, like swirls of vanilla ice cream.

"I'll let myself out," he says, not looking back.

In his car in the apartment complex parking lot, Professor Frank Harmon presses out the imagined creases in his clothes, in himself. He finds a comb in his back pocket and runs it through his hair in short strokes. His knuckles slide along the smoothness at the top edge of his forehead where his sandy blonde hair recedes, and he scowls at this detail, telling himself thirty-seven is not old enough for this.

The scent of jasmine chases him, and Frank thinks he can feel it on his lips, his tongue. He flings open the glove compartment and scavenges for the tin of breath mints he didn't intend for this, spilling six out onto his palm and popping them in his mouth all at once. By the time he pulls out of the parking lot, the jasmine is gone, replaced by a strong ghost scent he cannot identify.

He drives home, stopping only once at the Kroger four blocks from his house. When he returns to his car, the interior is still air-conditioner cool in the late August afternoon. He drops the brown paper bag in the passenger seat like a silent stranger. They didn't need the chicken breasts or the deli ham, and Sarah will turn her nose up at the frozen waffles, but Frank's only reason for stopping at the store was to use a cologne tester at the fragrance counter. Now he thinks he smells more like himself.

Frank sweats in his refrigerated car. He pulls into the driveway of his home, and the perfectness, the neatness of everything overwhelms him. Box hedges form lines up and down the block. Lawns are weedless, trimmed and verdant. Flowerbeds hold their soil in precise rectangles.

Even the trees grow straight. Nothing is allowed to stray. Holding the brown bag in front of him like a shield, Frank walks up the sidewalk to the front door. Sarah awaits him behind the storm door, but she won't step out onto the porch. At three months, her belly is beginning to show, and she has told him something is wrong in being blatant about her condition.

"Supper is almost ruined," she says. She starts to hug him but backs away as her eyes wander up and down his face. "You're sweaty. Get cleaned up for supper."

Frank knows the meal has been ready for exactly seventeen minutes. It is 6:17 p.m. He smiles a suffocating smile knowing she cannot touch the untidiness he has brought into the house. She is too neat, too clean.

Sarah takes the bag, peeking into it. Her hair slips forward like golden waves of silk ribbon, framing the roundness of her jaw line.

"We really don't need any of this. What took you so long? I called your office an hour ago, and you didn't answer."

Sarah saunters over to the kitchen. Frank doesn't miss the kiss he used to get when coming home, in fact he is happy she doesn't breathe him, just in case. The carpet under his feet feels as if it is falling away and holding him up at the same time.

"Long lines. I think the cash registers were down for a while, too."

His voice is as hollow as the house. The house is as hollow as his life. All are filled with things he thought, at one time, were supposed to be there.

*   *   *

In his office at the university, Frank stretches out in his chair, letting his head drop back and his eyes close. It is Friday at the end of his day, but he's not ready to go home. He is not ready to go anywhere else, either.

The door is locked, and every now and then he hears the muffled conversations of teachers or students passing by. The small room feels separate and neutral and his. Piles of student papers and folders cover his desk, bumping up against the computer and other knickknacks. Books crowd the shelves on two of the walls and sit in short stacks on the floor. Many of them are histories of local people, places and events of western North Carolina, written by colleagues. Plaques and awards hang on the walls, surrounding his diploma from Lakewood University, already more than ten years old.

He inhales with his entire body, trying to remember how he got where he

45

is. He wants to figure out where his former self went. Memories flood him, drown him. He is drinking tequila with a border runner in a Tijuana dive. He is camping under the stars in the Arizona desert. He is on a midnight watch for the moonbow at Cumberland Falls, Kentucky.

Everything is spontaneous, unplanned, exciting. Yet somewhere in all of that, the whisper of stability touches his ears. Some vision of what should come next imprints itself in his mind's eye.

*   *   *

The September nights are cold in Frank's house. The bedroom is coldest. Ever since she found out she was six weeks pregnant—almost two months ago—Sarah has become a restless and solitary sleeper, and this means Frank cannot sleep in peace either. Some nights he walks the length of the house, counting the steps away from his wife. Nothing clutters his path, and because Sarah insists on night-lights in all the rooms and the hallway, the house is not dark enough to hold surprises.

Frank ambles into the kitchen and doesn't bother to turn on the light. Everything is crisp and clean. The dish drainer and sinks are empty. The counter displays only necessary things.

The light of the waxing full moon sears the café curtains covering the window over the kitchen sink. For a moment Frank pictures another backyard, one with a rusting tool shed, weeds beginning to poke up around its base. Or maybe the other backyard would have a half-court for playing basketball with a few friends. Maybe the grass would need a clipping, but it wouldn't be so urgent that he couldn't do it the day after he threw a cookout for some neighbors.

Frank stands before the sink facing the window. He leaves the curtains drawn. He knows what is on the other side, and he knows how close it is. It is, in fact, all around him. He can feel the rending pull of the polished oak furniture, the glistening porcelain bathtub and the gleaming silver cutlery. Every part of his life is like that around here. His backyard is no different.

Keeping the silence intact, Frank opens the sliding glass door, descends the steps and stands on the back patio. The lawn is the sleek surface of a calm, deep sea, spreading out beyond vision. Frank feels the presence of the winter daphne behind him, beneath the kitchen window. It looms like a shadow.

They've only seen the winter daphne blossom once, earlier that year in late February. They planted the shrub a year ago after Sarah read about how it kept a good shape, didn't require pruning and bloomed in February or March.

When the tiny rose-pink blossoms first appeared, Sarah was pleased. She made Frank walk out with her in the freezing sunshine to look at the flowers, each petal as tiny as a baby's fingernail, she said. Frank was amazed at the strong fragrance of the plant. The sweet scent was too perfect, too appropriate.

Frank stares at the moon. Everything is silent except for the heartbeat in his ears, like drowning alone in a swimming pool.

*   *   *

He prepares to meet with her in his office before midterms in October. He feels his pulse in his throat as he cinches the knot of his tie closer to his neck. He buttons his dress coat. Though he is meeting with all his students to discuss their progress in his sophomore sociology class, this is decidedly different.

She is his one chance or his one mistake. He doesn't know which; it doesn't matter anymore. When she showed up in the front row of his fall class he remembered her from the summer semester, where she had hung careless flirtations and innuendo on him like new clothes. During the first week of the fall semester he had taken her invitation as if taking a dare. He feels the ghost of her on him, and he squirms in his suit.

As she arrives, he stands briefly before nodding at her to have a seat. He mumbles through her test grades, her quiz scores, her overall participation. She smirks at this last topic, and it is all he can do to keep his voice steady.

She is wearing an off-the-shoulder sweater that hangs in folds like the shelter of a baby's blanket. She leans back in her chair and twists her hair between her fingers. He finishes by telling her she has a solid B going into midterms. He avoids her eyes.

"If I made an A on midterms would that bring my overall average up? I'd really like an A in this course."

She leans forward. He hears the offer, but he looks for something safer in his student record book. His fingers stick to the pages as he flips them.

"It's all up to you," he says. "I've given you all the help I can."

He waits in the silence, not looking up. He wants to close his eyes and open them again to something else. He wants the understanding that evades him, the knowledge of reason. Or maybe he just wants everything to be easier.

"Don't sell yourself short, professor," she says, standing up.

The door creaks when she opens it to leave, and she doesn't shut it behind her. He looks up in time to see the butterfly float around the corner and disappear, chasing the trail of jasmine.

*　*　*

At Thanksgiving dinner at his parents' house, Frank gets drunk on the wine before the meal is served. He sits in the living room with his father, his younger brother, Thomas, and his brother-in-law, Wayne. Sarah and Frank's sister, Celia, whisper as they set the table.

Frank is not a loud, obnoxious drunk. He is the more dangerous introspective drunk. Every so often he slurs a cynical comment or wanders into another room. He constantly tugs at his shirtsleeves or tie, and none of his clothes seem to fit right. To Sarah's horror, Frank eventually rolls up the cuffs of his shirt.

Kate, his mother, has a hard time holding her smile in place when she sees him like this. She tries to smooth it over by telling everyone Frank has too much stress in his life. He has finals to think about, a new baby on the way, too much work. She speaks as if Frank is not in the room, and Frank's father, Mort, ignores the comments and talks over her to ask when the turkey will be done. For this interruption, Mort gets a reprimand from Kate, and the ensuing apology floats around the room like smoke from a warning signal, the

47

translation of which Frank is all too aware.

The conversation becomes a continuous buzz in his ears, and Frank finds himself standing up and wandering down the hall to his old bedroom, now the den. The family photos lining the hallway walls hang with precision, forming straight lines along their edges. The house is uncluttered and bright, and images flash behind Frank's eyes. He feels sick.

Frank leans against the doorframe of the den and peers into the room. Sunlight streams into the chamber, illuminating everything inside: the comfortable, overstuffed couch, the shiny cherry wood desk, the warm mahogany veneer of the table.

He crosses the room to the far wall plastered with photos. Photos of him on a donkey in the mountains near Monterrey, Mexico, on a beach in front of a lighthouse on Cape Cod, in the California hills with the Golden Gate Bridge in the background. Photos taken by friends or bystanders during lazy summers or spring breaks. Photos when he had no boundaries.

When he looks at these photos, Frank can see the carelessness in his frozen laughter. He can see the unconcerned youthfulness of his face. He sees no hint of the deep lines that appear near his eyes without warning these days. He thinks of days before the expectations, before the supposed-tos, before the invitations by students looking for better grades, before the life he somehow sank into.

"Everyone's ready. Are you?"

It's Sarah. Her voice is dispassionate. She stands at the door as if she cannot step into that part of the house, and maybe, Frank thinks, she will always be unable to take those steps.

*   *   *

By the time they leave, Frank is sober. Sarah doesn't speak until they are well out of Asheville. The roads to and from Willow Dale are barren. The highway glistens with wetness.

"I'm afraid for us," Sarah says, staring out the passenger-side window.

Frank feels the need for reassurance in her words. But he also detects an accusation. He realizes much too quickly he cannot respond to either.

"I am, too," he finally says.

"I thought we knew what we wanted. I thought this was part of it." Her left hand moves away from him to rest on her stomach.

"It was, until the doctors told us it would never happen. Anyways, it's more than that. You know that."

"I don't know what you want, Frank. I don't think you even know."

He lets it go at that. He doesn't have the words he needs. And those he has would be poison for someone.

*   *   *

At 1:30 a.m., Frank is drinking again. This is unusual for him, as he rarely drinks these days, and the only alcohol they have in the house is half a bottle of rum Sarah uses to make rum cakes.

In the living room, Frank flips through channels with the sound muted. He gulps his drink and thinks about his wife in the other room. Sarah is unaware

48

of what Frank is doing. She went to bed shortly after they got home, and the house allows isolation.

One, two, three drinks later, Frank can hear his thoughts better. They seep into his skin, his bones, his blood, even as the important things ooze out. He staggers into the kitchen, glass in hand, drink sloshing over the sides. He stands in the center of the room for a moment before walking over to the light switch and flipping it on.

He downs his drink and puts the glass on the counter. Condensation and spillage slide from the bottom of the glass. He grabs a cola from the refrigerator and mixes another drink, leaving the rum bottle on the counter. He picks up the empty glass of rum and puts it in the sink. In three gulps, Frank finishes the cola. He feels the tug. His thoughts are floating away. But he seizes one and holds it long enough to allow it to evolve into action.

Reaching over with an unsteady hand, Frank opens a kitchen drawer. The glittering silverware pulls him. His hand hovers over the forks, spoons, knives. Large knife. Carving knife. He holds it and wields it with something like familiarity.

The house is quiet and cold. Frank's thoughts are loud and hot.

Without regard for the silence, Frank steps onto the back patio. The tie is the first thing to go. With one hand, he snatches it off and tosses it onto the lawn. He peels off his shirt, slashing at it and rending it to shreds before discarding it. The heaviness in his chest rises up and emerges from him as laughter. In his undershirt, the November night is frigid and damp.

Frank walks to the winter daphne. He begins cutting at it with the knife, holding limbs with one hand and swiping at it with the other. He cuts his fingers more than once, but this is nothing to him. He is slicing leaves and shoots, perfectness and comfortableness.

"Take everything," he says, through ragged breath. "Take this. Take it all."

Sweat forms on Frank's brow, and his work becomes frenzied. He whittles away at the shrub until the evergreen is tattered and torn. Frank's laughter is interspersed with sobs.

"Frank? Frank, what are you doing?"

Sarah's voice comes at him from all directions. He can't find her at first. Then he sees her at the back door. When he looks at her, she covers her mouth with one hand and tries clutching together the front halves of her housecoat with the other. She drops the hand from her mouth to speak, and Frank can hear in her voice the tears threatening to escape.

"Frank, you're bleeding. What are you doing?"

"It's poison," Frank says, his voice bouncing off houses and shooting across lawns. "This is poison. It's dangerous."

"Frank, please come inside," Sarah says. Her voice is like a lesson recited to a child. "Put the knife down, and please come inside."

She hesitates, but then she moves past the doorframe, onto the top step. The shift confuses Frank, and now he wants to explain.

"It shouldn't be here."

"It's O.K., Frank. We'll take care of it later. Just please come in."

Something in him isn't listening, and Frank can't stop the space from expanding in his throat. He walks toward Sarah, and something clinks on the patio.

"I didn't mean to wake you."

"It's O.K., Frank," she says. "Come back to me."

"It's not O.K., Sarah. I don't know why …"

Frank squints at the bright kitchen light. He doesn't remember stepping inside with her. She hugs him, and he is aware of her disregard for the things he's capable of, the mess he can make of everything with his blood, his plant-stained hands.

"I'm sorry," he says, backing away from her. And he finds he is shivering but not cold. "I want to make everything better. I want to try to make everything better."

He looks into her eyes. Sarah is crying. And he feels things drifting back into him, important things he didn't know he missed.

"Don't say anything else, Frank. We can fix things. We'll fix everything."

And this, for him, is the most hopeful thing she has ever uttered.

* * *

They do not speak of the incident the next day. They are both different from themselves when they awake, yet they have been brought together. They rise just after ten o'clock to a day full of yellow light.

Everything from the night before is cleaned up or discarded. The debris, the clothes, the blood all vanish. The winter daphne is pruned and salvaged. It still appears healthy, and Frank thinks it is because the roots are so strong and deep. They will replace the shrub in the summer, Sarah tells him.

During the coming days, Frank tries twice to confess his indiscretion. Both times Sarah stops him before he can get it out. She tells him their future is the only thing that counts, and he thinks this is his penance, to keep his failure, his weakness, inside. He thinks she doesn't want this scar across all of them. He accepts this.

Three weeks before Christmas he has finished giving his last round of finals to his students. The building is silent on his last day, and he feels grateful for so many things he never planned on.

Driving home, Frank thinks of the apartment complex, an invitation. Outside the car, the gray clouds of twilight spit out specks of snow. He thinks of the smell of winter as he drives past the apartment where careless dustings on the asphalt swirl off the ground and die without notice.

* * *

On an afternoon glowing with newness in mid-March, Sarah rests in her bedroom. She rocks in a chair next to the bed holding their sleeping new daughter, and Frank stands in the doorway watching his future.

Sometimes it takes his breath away so completely he can't feel his own body. He knows what almost happened. He saw his child cling so hard to life she almost took her mother with her. The hours had been like a black light then, illuminating the things he valued, the things he wanted, the things he could not claim to deserve. And in that time, Frank felt his smallness, his helplessness, so much more than an infant.

Frank walks over to his family. He kneels beside the rocking chair, resting one arm on Sarah's shoulders and the other under his daughter.

"Hi, Daddy," Sarah says, smiling.

The word sounds good to Frank. He kisses Sarah, a soft feather against her cheek. He leans down and kisses his daughter, the realness of her and the bitterness of possibility mingling on his lips and sliding into his body. He feels grateful and new and high, and he wants to hold this moment forever. He wants the fear of what might have been to dissolve away, but it looms like a ghost in a lonely place near his heart. Everything feels better than he could have ever dreamed, and he knows it is.

Frank stands up. He doesn't want Sarah to see him like this.

Before walking away, he leans down one more time. The baby smells soft and warm and healthy when he kisses her.

Careful of the silence, Frank finds his wool coat in the hall closet. He steps outside, the daylight a kaleidoscope in his eyes. Everything looks different and fresh and wonderful, and his legs barely support him as he drops down on the porch steps. He sits there, crying in the frozen sun, the taste of possibilities fading from his lips, the scent of daphne overpowering him.

A DARK AND FEARSOME BEAST

We found it in the woods across the railroad tracks on the Fort Hardison military reservation. It made a noise that cut through the quiet September air and scared Aaron, but I thought it sounded like it was crying.

"What was that?" my little brother whispered. Frozen in mid-stride, Aaron clutched the large plastic pickle jar he had brought in case he found any frogs or salamanders; his eyes were as wide as the lid that covered it. "Alyssa, what was that?"

We were on the hiking trail coming back from Lost Cave. At 17, I was fulfilling my so-called responsibility as a young adult—as my parents were fond of calling me—by watching my kid brother for the afternoon. I edged forward.

I finally caught sight of it, entangled in a thorn bush to the right of the path ahead. It strained to free itself, each tug causing the spiked vines to press into its body. It whimpered each time this happened; it reminded me of a hurt cocker spaniel.

"Let's go around it," Aaron said, his voice cracking. "We'll be late for dinner, and dad will be mad."

"We can't leave it. I think it's hurt."

"It'll bite you; it has teeth," Aaron whispered. He walked backward two steps. "And it has long, sharp claws. I can see them. Come on, let's go."

I ignored him. For a fifth-grader, he was a complete wuss. In contrast, my dad calls me the biggest tomboy in Ordinary, maybe in the whole state of Kentucky.

The thing watched me as I approached it, its long, thin tail twitching a little. The dark creature looked like a lost shadow. By the time I got right up to it, it had stopped whimpering.

I glanced back at Aaron. He fiddled with what I call his Jesus jewelry, a buddy bracelet he had gotten in Sunday school from his friend Paul, who lives across the street. Paul's father is a preacher at Ordinary First Baptist Church just down the street, and Aaron is like a personal project to him and his wife. Thankfully, everyone has already given up on me.

When I knelt next to the thorn bush, I could feel my pulse in my throat. The animal made me nervous. It looked like it could be very dangerous, even though it acted as if it wouldn't hurt me. It appeared small and inconspicuous from a distance but large and very strong as I got closer. It constantly seemed to change its face.

I carefully untangled the thing from the briars, keeping my eyes on it the whole time. I remember not wanting it to touch me, but I'm not sure why.

As I pulled the last briar branch away from it, I stepped back. It slithered into the clearing and faced me. The thing confused me, but I wanted to understand it.

"Let's go now," Aaron said. "We can still be home in time to wash up for dinner if we cut through Mrs. Miller's backyard."

I didn't like the idea of cutting through old Mrs. Miller's yard, because if she caught us she would want to gossip or have us go in and visit, and her house always smelled like a hospital room. I agreed only because I didn't know what else to do. I didn't know the creature would follow us.

* * *

We stopped at the edge of the woods and turned to face the thing. Aaron took the lid off the pickle jar and handed it to me.

"What am I supposed to do with this?" I said. "It's too big to fit in here."

The thing took a few steps toward us; it was maybe 10 feet away. It seemed to stare at the jar, so I put the open container down on its side, not really knowing why.

The creature was smaller now, and it scurried into the jar. I felt a little nervous when the thing was in my hands, regardless of the plastic barrier. The animal felt weightless. I thought I would never know its true nature.

Aaron wanted to put the lid on the jar, but I pushed him away. I knew it wouldn't die, but I thought it would do something desperate if it thought it was trapped.

We left the woods and crossed Spring Street, cutting through the backyards of the houses on the other side. As we made our way across the first back-yard I was surprised to see a new family was moving into the Sullivan's house that had been empty all summer. For a brief moment, memories of Trina flashed in my mind. I mentally brushed them away.

We could see the Atlas moving van and a cream-and-white Lexus in the side gravel driveway, and we caught a glimpse of a man and two kids taking things from the trunk of the car. Two moving men were unloading things from the van.

The man and the kids had deep brown skin and were dressed in long, loose garments. One of the kids was a teen-age girl about my age, and the other was a little girl maybe a couple of years younger than Aaron.

I told Aaron to hurry up because they hadn't seen us. We jogged across the back of the lot and onto old Mrs. Miller's yard. We unexpectedly ran into Mrs. Miller standing at the shed near the back of her property. She wore a floral muumuu that swallowed her up. She was putting a padlock on the shed doors, which didn't make sense to me since I've never seen Mrs. Miller lock anything in her life, even her front door. She always kept her place open for visitors and neighbors.

"Alyssa and Aaron Wright!" she said, jumping like we had startled her. "You kids know better than to sneak around other people's property."

"Sorry," I said, pressing the jar under my left arm. "We're late for dinner."

Mrs. Miller clicked the padlock shut and peered at us over her wire-framed glasses. Her wrinkled and hollow cheeks showed hints of pink. She didn't say anything for a moment, but her eyes kept glancing between us and her new neighbors.

"Get along then but keep an eye out," she said. "This town is going to the dogs."

53

With that, she shuffled off toward her house. The muumuu hung off her and flapped like a flag in the wind, and she looked like some weird skeleton animated in slow motion.

* * *

I put the thing in the cellar while Aaron let dad know we were back. Mom and dad hardly go down there except during spring cleaning when they store stuff and throw things out. It smelled moldy and forgotten down there.

When I let it out of the jar it grew bigger. It seemed happy to lurk in the background, blending in with the shadows. I wanted to leave the bare light bulb on, more for me than for it. I didn't like the idea of not knowing where it was or how close it could be to me. But I turned off the light like I'm supposed to.

Since it was Thursday, Dad had made dinner. Dad cooks on weekdays because mom works at the Five Star convenience store until 9 p.m. On Fridays and Saturdays mom works the morning shift because dad told her he didn't want her working at night on the weekends. That's when the drunks and nutcases come out, he said.

I didn't sleep well that night. I had e-mailed Trina before going to bed; I'd look for her reply the next day. Trina used to let me go over to her house and just hang out. I missed her and hated how her parents kicked her out and then moved to Tennessee. But Trina managed to do okay working third shift as a stocker at Target. We e-mail each other a couple of times a week, and she always tells me I'm living in the wrong place. Trina says Ordinary isn't a town for people who want to grow.

Before I went to bed Aaron had asked me a lot of stupid questions that bothered me. He wondered what the creature was and wondered if it would howl at night like a dog left outside that wants in. He asked if it would sneak into our rooms and suck our brains out. I told him he didn't have anything to worry about, but he didn't get it.

Mostly, I thought about what I had seen that day. It scared me.

Adults talk about monsters as if they don't really exist, but I know better. I caught my first glimpse of a monster that day. Monsters are real. Monsters are everywhere.

* * *

I met my new neighbor the following Monday at school during lunch. Me and my best friend, Amy Basham, had just gone through the slop line. The girl sat alone at the far end of one of the tables in the cafeteria; her multi-colored print blouse reached all the way down to her knees, and she wore matching loose pants.

As Amy and I approached the table, I heard Matt Frakes and his buddies, Danny and Bill, making cracks about her at the other end, something stupid about camels. She stared straight ahead as she ate. She looked stiff, like she was trying to create a force field to keep things out. We sat down across from her, and I glared at Matt and the others.

"Don't pay any attention to them," I said. "They're a result of inbreeding."

The girl's brown eyes glanced up at me for a split second, and the

54

corners of her mouth flinched upward. She had a smile that looked new.

I pulled the top bun off my hamburger. A chemical scent rose from the patty, and my nose couldn't help but wrinkle. I tore open a packet of catsup and squirted it onto the patty.

Amy and I offered introductions as she pushed her salad around with her fork. I told her about my family—my dad, the loan officer at First Citizens Bank; my mom, the convenience store clerk; my bratty little brother—and Amy told her about her mother, who works in Elizabethtown on a production line that makes car dashboards. The new girl told us her name was Daliya Mahmood and that she was a senior, like us. Her father was a professor at Elizabethtown Community and Technical College, and her mother was a doctor at Hardin Memorial Hospital. Her little sister, Miah, was in the third grade.

While we talked, Matt Frakes cupped one hand around his mouth and made crude comments, straightening up afterward as if he thought he was fooling someone. He and his buddies laughed. Matt's white trash girlfriend, Theresa, had plopped down beside him. She wore trampy make-up—too bright and too thick for her pale complexion and fake-blonde hair—and her tight T-shirt clung to her big boobs. She used ugly orange lipstick that made her mouth look like talking wedges of pumpkin rind. Theresa's equally repulsive girlfriend, Nikki, sat beside her, her face so drawn and hard it could have belonged to someone twice her age with half her hardships. Nikki constantly pushed back her stringy brown hair with her long purple fingernails.

Matt said things like "go home" or "terrorist." My face burned from embarrassment and anger. I hate jerks like Matt.

Me and Amy kept telling Daliya that Matt and his friends were morons, that not everyone was like him. She seemed like she was trying to believe me. When the bell rang for next period we walked out of the lunchroom with Daliya. As we stepped into the hallway, the crude comments resumed. But this time the voice was female.

*   *   *

The creature wouldn't eat anything we gave it. I sensed its hunger, but we couldn't seem to figure out what it fed off. Aaron or I would go to the cellar after dinner and offer it leftovers or scraps, but it would only sniff at the food then turn away. With all the time I was spending with Aaron, mom and dad thought we were bonding or something.

Mom keeps telling me how lucky Aaron and I are because we have two parents and live in our own house, not like the people who live in Durham Mobile Home Park or the black people who live in the apartments on Locust Street. It always bothered me when she said things like that. Dad never said anything, but I've seen him around people of lower income or a different race; he acts different. Lately it has become harder for me to ignore such things.

The day after we put the creature in the cellar, Aaron hurried home after school to check on it. He had to make sure mom and dad hadn't found it. They hadn't. That weekend we kept a close eye on the cellar, which meant one of us had to stay home at all times. Then on Monday, we started to worry again that mom or dad would find it while we were at school, but they never did.

*　*　*

Amy and I ate lunch with Daliya the rest of the week. By Thursday, we were all like old friends. We had all gotten pretty good at ignoring Matt, Theresa and the others.

Daliya was a big U2 fan, like us, but she also liked alternative stuff, like Bowling for Soup and The Foo Fighters. She told us how she sometimes just wanted to wear blue jeans and a T-shirt instead of her shalwar kameez. Her family moved from her hometown of Lahore, Pakistan, to the United States five years ago. They moved to Ordinary from New York because they didn't like the big city, especially after 9-11.

We told her about the Kentucky Derby and the UK Wildcats, neither of which me nor Amy had much interest in. Mostly we told her how mind-numbingly boring Ordinary was, how the nearest Wal-Mart was almost 10 miles away, how the only fast food restaurant in town was the Dairy Queen on 31-W, how everyone had to leave town to buy clothes unless they wanted to buy them in a thrift store or at a yard sale.

Thursday during lunch the three of us decided to meet and walk home together after school. We agreed to meet at Daliya's locker because it was closest to the exit doors at the end of the hallway. Amy and I had World Geography as our last class, so we walked together to meet Daliya. We ran into her on the way.

"I want to see Ordinary," Daliya said. "My parents hardly go anywhere here in town. They go to Elizabethtown or Louisville."

"That's because there's nothing here," Amy said.

"Everyone takes their hometown for granted. In Lahore, during the festival of kites, the sky is filled with shape and color, like a kaleidoscope. I took Basant for granted, and now I miss it."

"What do you want to see?" I asked.

"I want to see everything in a typical small town—"

When Daliya stopped short, I thought she was just being hesitant about confiding in us. She had stopped in her tracks, and the expression on her face was hard to read. Then I heard Amy gasp.

I followed her gaze to Daliya's locker. The words, "Go home Arab terrorist" were scrawled on the gray metal surface in ugly orange lipstick.

*　*　*

Daliya was quiet on our walk home. Amy and I had tried to get her to report the graffiti to the principal. We knew, of course, whose lipstick was on Daliya's locker door. We both wanted to beat the crap out of Theresa, and that says a lot for Amy since she's basically not a violent person. But Daliya said she didn't want to make an issue of it. Instead, she had used a Kleenex from her purse to wipe the lipstick off her locker door, though it left an ugly smudge.

We walked Daliya home first and met her father. He was getting his briefcase out of the backseat of the Lexus. He was nice enough, I guess, but he

56

seemed like he was in a hurry. He shook our hands and told us he was glad
to meet us, then took Daliya in the house and told us goodbye.

As Amy and I crossed the street to go the two blocks down where she lived,
I glanced over at Mrs. Miller's house. I saw the edge of the drawn living
room curtains flutter. The front door was closed.

*   *   *

Sometimes the creature seemed to appear out of nowhere. Aaron and I
would be standing in the center of the cellar, checking on it, and I would
look down, and there it would be, right next to me. Or it would materialize
directly behind Aaron without him knowing it, its face hovering right over
Aaron's shoulder. It would always raise its muzzle and sniff the air, like a
bloodhound relying on scent rather than sight. I didn't like the fact that it
could get so close without me knowing it. It never touched us or hurt us, but
it always seemed to be ready to.

Aaron wanted to name it. He decided it was male. He thought Shadow
sounded like a cool name, so he would call for it whenever we checked on it
after school. The thing didn't respond to the name, and I never expected it to.

But I guess that bothered me, too. It seemed to be too wild and unpredict-
able to be controlled. It made me wonder if we really had any control over it
at all.

*   *   *

One Saturday afternoon, at the end of September, Daliya, Amy and me
went to Ordinary Cafe. Mrs. Tate, who runs the place, stood behind the
counter ringing up a customer. She remembered me when we walked in and
told us to take a seat wherever we wanted. The place wasn't very full, just a
few people on barstools at the counter and a few scattered here and there at
tables.

We chose a booth across from the end of the counter. I sat next to Daliya,
and Amy sat across from us. A waitress not much older than us took our
orders.

When our waitress brought us our Cokes, I heard a guy at the counter
mumble something, just barely audible. I distinctly heard him say the word
"Arab."

The man turned and stared at us, and I realized it was Reverend Vertrees,
Paul's father. He wore a white long-sleeved shirt and tie. I wanted to say
something, but his eyes had fire in them, and I suddenly knew him better
than before. Mrs. Tate walked over to him with a pot of coffee and a cup.

"Fill 'er up, Hal?" Mrs. Tate asked, setting the cup in front of him.

"Didn't know you served terrorists, Ruth," Rev. Vertrees said, nodding
toward us.

I gritted my teeth. From the corner of my eye I could see Daliya stiffen,
but I was glad to see she raised her chin and didn't look down. Amy muttered "asshole" under her breath.

Mrs. Tate stiffened, too, one balled fist on her hip. I hadn't noticed the
murmur of conversation in the diner until just then, when it all stopped.

57

At first I wasn't sure how Mrs. Tate would react. But I saw how the knuckles of the hand on her hip turned white and how the carafe in her other hand shook. Her red face looked ready to explode.

"We don't serve terrorists, Hal, so I won't be serving you. Get out of my diner."

"The Bible tells us—"' Rev. Vertrees started to say.

"I said get out," Mrs. Tate said. "Now."

Rev. Vertrees grumbled as he got off the stool. He stopped for a second and turned toward our booth. All three of us stared back at him. Two other men—one from the counter and another from a booth next to ours—stood and faced Rev. Vertrees.

"Damned Arabs!" Rev. Vertrees said before turning and heading for the door.

"Out, Hal, or I'm calling the cops."

We watched him as he walked out into the parking lot and drove off. It was like keeping an eye on a mad dog, unwilling to give it the advantage of surprise.

*   *   *

One Monday after school, about a week later, I found dad at the kitchen table going over some bills. I hurried to my bedroom upstairs and threw my books on the bed. Aaron wasn't in his room across the hall, so I made my way back downstairs.

"Your brother's out back with Paul and that other kid, Rodney or Robbie or whatever his name is," dad said, as if reading my mind.

I stopped in my tracks. For one thing, I was surprised Paul was allowed to come over to my house, seeing as how I consorted with terrorists. All I knew about Rodney was that he was pretty rough around the edges; his whole family was like that. I had a bad feeling.

"I'll go check on them," I finally said. Dad just mumbled something.

When I got to the backyard, I found the cellar door open, as I had feared. From the doorway I could hear voices, and I could tell the boys were at the far end of the room.

I swallowed hard and poked my head in. My eyes squinted as they tried to adjust to the dim lighting. I called for Aaron in the calmest voice I could manage.

I was suddenly afraid the creature might attack Aaron's friends while I stood there. When Aaron answered, I went in and looked around. He was moving some boxes.

"Aaron, what are you doing?" I yelled, trying not to sound as pissed off as I was. "You know you're not supposed to be down here."

Aaron swung around to face me. His mouth was wide open, like he was waiting for words to fall out.

"Come on," I said, pointing to the door. "Everyone out."

"My parents said if that Arab girl's here I got to go home," Paul said, frowning.

"Yeah," Rodney chimed in. "My Mom says the only good Arab is a dead one."

58

I took a deep breath to still my trembling body. Then I repeated my order
for them to leave.

But before anyone could move, the thing flew across the room and landed
near the foot of the steps. It skulked near the staircase for a few seconds
before making its way toward us, noiselessly, like a black cat on the scent of a
mouse.

"Cool!" Paul said, his voice wavering. "What is it?"

The creature blended into the shadows and emerged behind Rodney. It
sniffed the air and rubbed against the back of his legs. Rodney jumped away
from it and turned around. The animal somehow looked larger and darker
before it darted away.

"Kill it!" Rodney said. "It attacked me."

"No, it didn't," Aaron shouted. "Shadow hasn't ever tried to hurt anybody."

I told the boys the creature was a secret and started to herd them up the
stairs, but then something happened that hadn't happened before. From the
darkened corner of the cellar, a pair of large orange eyes appeared, glowing
like miniature setting suns.

"That thing is evil," Rodney said. "It wants to kill us."

"Everyone up the stairs," I said, waving them on. I didn't have to argue
with them. They ran up the steps while I faced the back of the cellar. The
unblinking orange orbs watched me, as if waiting for me to stumble. I studied the fiery points of light, thinking maybe I could read them, see beyond
the outside to what caused them to burn like that. But all I felt was a large-
ness, like a deep well of history I couldn't touch.

* * *

When I stepped out into our backyard, Rodney and Paul were gone. Aaron
was fidgeting by the swing set in a way he does whenever he's done something wrong and gets caught.

"They said they wouldn't tell anyone," he said.

I scowled. I felt like a parent, and I didn't like it.

"We can't keep it anymore," I said. "We have to let it go in the woods
where we found it. Maybe it won't follow us this time."

It was Aaron's turn to scowl. He looked disappointed and hurt. I don't
think he knew how dangerous things were. He looked at Shadow like many
other people might, as if it was some formless, vague notion without sub-
stance. But I didn't see it that way anymore. I knew it was something to
guard against, and now I wanted it as far away from me as possible.

* * *

While we were having dinner—spaghetti, dad's specialty—the doorbell
rang. From the kitchen I couldn't see dad or who he was talking to, but I
could hear something in his voice that told me he wasn't happy. My throat
closed up, and I stared at Aaron. We both stopped eating.

"Alyssa! Aaron! Come here. Now!"

Rodney's mother filled the frame of the front door. She stood with her
hands on her hips. She had tucked her oily hair under a bandana; Rodney

stood behind her. No one knows who or where Rodney's father was.

"Rodney says you two are keeping a wild animal in the cellar. Is that true?"

"Don't sugarcoat it," Miss Darnell snapped. "Your kids let a wild animal attack my boy."

Dad stared at me. I could feel Aaron move behind me.

"It didn't attack him," I said. I couldn't look anyone in the eye.

That's when Rodney started going on about how dangerous Shadow was, and his mother started threatening to sue dad, and then Paul and his parents came over and started giving dad the third degree, and everyone except me was talking at the same time until dad agreed to get rid of Shadow. Aaron's eyes got watery, and dad told us to show him where Shadow was.

All the parents insisted on going with us, but they made Rodney and Paul stay behind. When we got to the back of the house, the cellar door stood wide open, and we could see the light was on inside. I turned to Aaron but didn't say anything.

When we were all in the cellar, Aaron called for Shadow. Like usual, the creature didn't respond. But this time it was different. We searched the cellar, but it was obvious that Shadow was gone. He was loose, and I knew he hadn't gone back to the woods.

*   *   *

That night I awoke just after midnight to the sound of a police siren. When I opened my eyes to the darkness, everything looked the same, and I realized my eyes had been open the whole time. The siren screamed like a banshee past our house but didn't die down much. I didn't have to get up and look. I knew its destination.

I lay there staring at the ceiling, watching the pulsating blue lights bounce around my room. Everything looked distorted, shapes elongated and shortened by tricks of light and shadow. Something caused me to start trembling, and my face became wet. After a while the blue was gone, and darkness once again dropped over my eyes like a black veil.

*   *   *

Daliya and her family weren't physically hurt, but they had to replace the living room window because a brick went through it. The police didn't arrest anybody, even though everyone knew Matt Frakes had something to do with it.

A surprising number of people in town voiced their disapproval of what had happened. At school, the day after the incident, a lot of students suddenly became friends with Daliya. Though some were genuinely upset and sympathetic, it was obvious that many of them didn't really care about Daliya or her family. They just wanted to be part of something that people in Ordinary were talking about.

"This town is full of hypocrites," I told Daliya as we walked home from school that day.

"I don't blame the town," she told me. "It's everywhere. My parents are angry, not scared like before. I just want to live a normal life."

60

Her voice had something in it. Her eyes had lost something. The town around us breathed puffs of air, like a sleeping dragon.

I didn't say anything else. Daliya could easily have been one of those missing or runaway children on those mass-mailed postcards: Have you seen me?

The October leaves crunched under our feet. Patchy gray clouds spat rain on us.

I went home. I didn't eat much of my dinner, but dad and Aaron didn't seem to notice. I sent an e-mail to Trina before crawling into bed. The night edged over us and covered the sparkling eyes in a heaven that turned its head away from us.

*   *   *

The Rolling Z Truck Stop on KY 31-W—which skirts Ordinary to the west—is also a Greyhound bus stop. The bus picks up passengers and takes them out of town, heading north to Louisville and on to Cincinnati or south to Elizabethtown where it hits the Blue Grass Parkway and heads to Lexington or takes I-65 to Bowling Green or even Nashville.

In June, a week after graduation and two weeks before my 18th birthday, I bought a ticket to Louisville with savings from my allowance. I had arranged to stay with Trina. I told mom and dad Amy was letting me stay over for the weekend. Amy didn't want me to go, but she understood.

Things had gotten better for Daliya the past few months, but it was too late as far as I was concerned. And Daliya is stronger and more forgiving than I am. For me, everything—the holidays, my graduation, my birthday—had been tinged with a darkness like the brown spots on rotting fruit.

As the bus pulled away from Ordinary, I closed my eyes. The road hummed and clicked underneath me, and my heart drummed a quick beat. I thought how Ordinary should have been the type of small town where people wanted to live, where everyone knew each other and helped each other. But that was an illusion. Ordinary was like that: a broken promise. I have no illusions about Louisville, so it will be different.

I'm not like I used to be. I'm growing, and I know why it hurts so much.

I have seen the monster. It has teeth like jagged triangles of stained glass. It is a wild creature that can never be tamed, a beast without reason or logic. It is always ravenous and ready to feed, a desperate thing with lifeless, sightless eyes. It is a dark and fearsome beast.

FEATHERED FRIEND

I hate that bird. God, how I hate that stupid bird!

But I couldn't get rid of him without looking suspicious, and I didn't want that. No, things were tricky enough without having to explain Mr. Harry's absence. There would be too many questions if I got rid of that bird. I had to bide my time, suffer that squawking beast till the end of its natural life, make it look like I had some sentimental attachment to it.

When I strangled that adulterous mouse of a woman who—for six years—I called my wife, I wanted to do the same to her stupid bird. I don't know how I kept myself from it; I was so blind with rage. I'm sure his neck would have snapped in my hands rather easily—

But I'm getting ahead of myself. I should start at the beginning, just as you asked. Then, when you print my story, everything will be cleared up, because there have been some false reports. There have been so many false reports.

It's true that I'm somewhat "bookish," as one television report described me. What a shock. Imagine that: a high school literature teacher of nine years being "bookish." Unfortunately, these days people look at you funny if you're more interested in Henry IV Part II than Friday 13th Part 30. I don't care.

All I cared about was Leslie. And I once truly believed she cared about me.

I remember the first time I saw her, like it was yesterday. It was eight years ago on a Saturday afternoon at the public library branch on Third Street. She worked as a library aide, and she was shelving Poe's Tales of Mystery and Imagination.

She nearly jumped out of her skin when I came up behind her to ask her for help with the copier. I apologized for scaring her, but she laughed and said she was just jittery. I hardly heard her explanation, something about an old boyfriend who wouldn't leave her alone. I was so entranced with that laugh, that smile. Her hair, the color of wet sand, dangled about her waist, and her eyes, the faint blue of a hazy summer sky, held a certain kindliness.

Some people would say it was love at first sight. That's what I used to think. Not anymore. Love at first sight is nothing more than the desperate act of a lonely heart. I see that now. When I look back, I can see the long list of failures that led me to that hopeless relationship; I realize how much I wanted something stable and real, something I could call my own. What a fool I was!

Every Saturday for three months I returned to that library, always with some excuse to talk to her. And she was never rude or inattentive. For a 26-year-old, she was fairly well read. We were able to discuss literature, and I pretended I had enjoyed the contemporary works we had both read.

Don't think I didn't notice how some of the guys looked at her. I knew what they were thinking. But when I was there with her, I made sure they knew what I was thinking, too. I think she appreciated that, in some unspoken way.

I was five years her senior, and, at first, I thought this might cause some problems. But she seemed to be enamored of the fact that I had been places, done things, that I had a respectable job and my own house in the country. Granted it isn't much, but the small frame house is nice enough. It's located in a quiet, secluded area in the eastern part of the county, so we had our privacy. And the city is only 25 minutes away.

* * *

You didn't hear it? You really should be more observant; you're a journalist, after all. Don't they teach you to watch and listen? I guess you were wrapped up in my story, huh? Ha, ha! A captive audience!

Anyway, where was I? Oh, yeah, right after we started seeing each other. We were married just two years after we met, in June. Yeah, I know, but she wanted that traditional June wedding thing, and I had no problems with it. The ceremony was small. None of my family showed up, but that was no surprise. My only brother and his family were off somewhere in Europe and sent some cheesy silverware with a scribbled note of apology for their absence. Mom has been dead for almost 15 years now, and dad was probably at home drinking his disability pay and wondering when the wedding was and how he could have misplaced that invitation. Two members of the faculty showed up, and one of my neighbors made it.

Leslie's family and friends did a better job. About a dozen people sat on Leslie's side. I had met her parents, Gene and Sylvia, and her older brother, Todd, and her younger sister, Jennifer, a year earlier, when Leslie and I first got engaged. Even then, I could tell Todd would be trouble. For some reason, that brother of hers looked at me like a convenience store clerk eyeing a potential shoplifter.

But I did my best to stay on good terms with her family. I know how important family can be.

For the first few years, things went well. Leslie and I spent all our off hours together. She loved books, and I loved old books, so we went to flea markets, yard sales and antiquarian bookstores together.

We used to spend hours at The Book Shelf, a used and rare bookstore. They had old editions of Hemingway and Steinbeck and others, not true firsts but second and third impressions of first editions. I almost popped 50 bucks for an old edition of Call of the Wild, you know, London. That had been one of my favorites when I was in high school. Leslie said I should get it, and maybe I should have, but I decided against it, and the next time we went there it had been sold.

Sometimes I'd find a good old book at a thrift store for 50 cents, knowing it was worth much more. I'd always buy it with misgivings.
"I feel guilty about doing this," I'd whisper to Leslie.

"The only time you should feel guilty about something is if you know you're doing something wrong," she told me. "And there's nothing wrong with what you're doing. If you didn't buy their books, someone else would.

63

They just want to sell their items so they can get the money they need to help others. Besides, all their items are donated, so it's not like they're losing anything."

I knew she was right. And she had a point about guilt. The only thing that substantiates guilt is the realization of wrongful intent.

So we enjoyed our outings. And we did things as a couple. That was nice. We ate at good restaurants and visited museums. We watched sunsets and gazed at the stars. In the winter we would stand in the grove of trees at the back of the property and watch snowflakes fall through the bare limbs. Sounds kind of sickening, doesn't it? But I really liked doing that stuff.

And our house slowly became a home, a place I looked forward to coming to at the end of the day. Leslie planted flowers and vegetables. She bought comfortable furniture and warm quilts. We talked about having a family.

I wanted children. And she had told me early in our relationship that she did, too. But the timing never seemed right. Something always got in the way. For a while, it was a matter of finances. Then it was our ages, the fact that we were already in our 30s.

And just when we decided to go ahead and try, Leslie's sister was diagnosed with breast cancer. During Jennifer's two-year battle, Leslie seemed distant. Not that I couldn't understand this, but things just got so stressful.

Once—on the morning that Jennifer was to go in for her first treatment—Todd came over. Leslie and I had planned on going to the hospital, but Todd wanted us all to go together. He was obviously distraught, and I tried to say things that would calm him, but it didn't help.

"I don't know what I'd do if we lost her," he told Leslie. "This is something I can't protect her from. I can't do anything."

The better Jennifer got, the more Todd seemed to drop by. At first I thought Jennifer's ordeal was just making him more grateful for family.

But the more I thought about it, the more I thought he was trying to act as Leslie's protector. Like she needed one. And if he didn't drop by, he'd call. We'd exchange a few civilities; then he'd ask to talk to Leslie.

I didn't mind. A family should be close.

* * *

I'm getting to it. Do you have a cigarette? They said you might have cigarettes. Thanks. I don't really smoke much.

She got that bird a couple of years ago. It had been a store mascot for a while, but it kept getting stolen. I don't know why anyone would want to steal that thing; it chattered incessantly. I guess they just decided to get rid of it before it got stolen again.

They called it Mr. Harry, so Leslie didn't actually give it that stupid name. It would say things like "Mr. Harry is a pretty bird" and "Talk to me." It drove me nuts.

But Leslie loved that cockatoo. She taught it a few more phrases, and it learned fast. Too fast, as far as I'm concerned.

I got to where I could ignore him. And if he got too noisy, I would just cover the cage, and he would usually be quiet.

Leslie said she liked having Mr. Harry around whenever I wasn't there. I

64

did some tutoring some evenings, and she said Mr. Harry made her feel like she wasn't alone.

I don't know how she could have ever felt alone when she was constantly inviting people to the house. She would have neighbors over sometimes when I got home from work. Or she'd have a girlfriend from the library over for dinner. Once a month or so, her parents or her sister would visit. And Todd made it over once or twice a week.

But none of that really bothered me. And then there was Warren.

What a name, huh? Warren. He ran The Book Shelf, that used bookstore we used to go to all the time. I always thought that—being into literature and all—he should have changed his last name to Peace. Get it? Warren Peace! Ha, ha! I thought it was amusing, but Leslie always rolled her eyes at that. I think she started losing her sense of humor over the years.

We had never really stopped going to The Book Shelf, but in the past couple of years we went less often. About two months ago, Leslie renewed her interest in going there. I was happy at first. We had gotten into kind of a rut.

But she seemed to always plan her visits to the store when I couldn't go. She would plan it on a night I had a tutoring session or when I had some school function.

Then there were the calls. Sometimes Warren had the nerve to call when I was around, and when I would answer the phone, he would make nervous conversation. But he always ended up asking for Leslie. Other times, I would catch her talking to Warren on the phone, and she would play it off like she was asking about the store's business hours or something equally unbelievable. I started to suspect the "business" she was really interested in, and it had nothing to do with books.

I began catching her in more and more lies over the past few weeks. I never confronted her with her inaccuracies. Oh, no, that's what she wanted, so she could say I was the one with the insecurities.

Then last Tuesday I came home and heard her talking on the phone. She finished her conversation in whispers, and I didn't say anything about it. Later that night, during dinner, she told me she would be late coming home Wednesday. She had some "errands" to run. Can you believe that? She really thought I'd buy that!

Well, I made a special point to track her after work without her knowing. She got off work at six, like clockwork. She was anxious, so eager to see Warren. That's a fact. You can check it out. She went straight to The Book Shelf, in broad daylight!

I waited in my car half a block down from the store. I waited for 20 minutes, but I couldn't bear it. I couldn't stay and watch her humiliate me in public. Everything I had felt for her caught on fire and seared me from the inside out.

I drove home and waited. Mr. Harry wouldn't shut up, and I couldn't bear to listen to him, to listen to the things she taught him, words she had given him, just more things she had given to someone else. I must have covered that cage to make him shut up, but I don't remember much until Leslie stepped in the door about seven-thirty.

"Where have you been?" I asked her. Just like that. Calm. Not suspicious.

Calm.

"Oh, I just swung by the craft store to look for a cross-stitch pattern, but they didn't have anything I liked," she said.

Liar! Liar! My mind throbbed with the word, like a headache.

I jumped up from the chair. I couldn't speak at first. Can you blame me? I was so angry, so betrayed.

When I grabbed her, she dropped her purse. I pushed her against the door.

"Liar!" I screamed at her. "Liar!"

She said I was hurting her, but I didn't care. My hands found her throat, and I can remember feeling her pulse under my fingers, smelling her perfume that used to be just for me. Her mouth gaped, but she made only gurgling noises.

"I won't let you cheat on me! I'll kill you!" I said this over and over as I watched her eyes roll back into her head.

I felt hot, like I was burning with fever. I saw nothing but her face and my hands around her neck. I don't know how long it took. Everything was different. Time. Place. Memory. All of it was different.

I looked around. It was dark in the house; it was night outside. How does that happen? How can a person lose track of time like that?

I knew what I had to do, though. This would look bad if I reported what had happened. No one would believe me; no one had seen her betrayal. They would think I didn't have a reason. But I did.

So I went out back and dug her a place in that grove of trees. Fitting really. We had spent so much time there. It was like spending time with her there again.

*   *   *

It's okay. I'm okay. They don't like me to get worked up like that. Sorry for the interruption, but they say I should take deep breaths when that happens.

But I'm okay now. Don't be nervous. It's not like I'm a real killer.

Anyway, like I was saying, I buried her out back. I drove her car to the library parking lot and took a cab home. I reported her missing late that night, and the cops said I should call back the next afternoon if she hadn't shown up by then. She didn't, and I did.

And you know what that means. I had to call her family. I had to. That's what any loving husband would do.

Todd got there right after the cops did. He was out of control, a madman. He had it in his mind that I had something to do with her disappearance. He didn't even know about her.

One of the cops made him sit down. The other one started asking questions, like when I last saw her and what she was wearing.

I was doing just fine. Had my story straight and everything.

I had said good-bye to her on Wednesday morning before work. She was supposed to run some errands after she got off work at six. But she never made it home.

The officer questioning me asked if we had gotten into a fight. What was that supposed to mean? I couldn't believe what he was implying. I told him we most certainly had not gotten into a fight.

Then I heard it. It was faint at first.

"Liar!"

I turned and looked around the room. No one moved.

"We had a wonderful relationship," I said. I wasn't about to let the comment go unanswered. "We loved each other."

"Liar!"

I stood up. The officer near me put his hand on his holster. What kind of game was he playing?

"Take it easy," he said.

I said, "You take it easy! You're the one calling me a liar! What makes you think you would know—"

But I stopped because I realized whose voice it was. I was so stupid.

"I'll kill you!" Mr. Harry screamed.

"Shut up!" I yelled. I couldn't keep the anger out of my voice.

Then I calmed myself down. They were all staring at me.

"That bird is always spouting nonsense," I told them.

My mouth felt suddenly dry. My legs felt weak. I glanced at the covered birdcage.

"Excuse me?" The officer gave his partner a look. I knew that look. He couldn't hide his suspicion.

"I just—"

"I won't let you cheat on me!" Mr. Harry screeched.

"Shut up, you stupid bird!"

I took a few steps toward the cage. The officer stopped me.

"Are you okay?" he asked.

Like nothing was wrong. Like that bird wasn't incriminating me.

"I'm fine!"

"I'll kill you! I'll kill you!"

"Don't listen to him. I didn't say that! I don't know where that bird picked that up."

The officer tried making me sit down. But Mr. Harry wouldn't stop. He kept on and on, louder and louder, saying those words, those words I had spoken when I killed her, and I could see it in their eyes, all of them, laughing secretly at me, playing this game with me, acting like they couldn't hear that wretched bird squawking and screeching, telling them what I did, accusing me, tormenting me with those words, those words, those words I said when—

"I killed her!" I screamed it. I shouted over Mr. Harry. "I killed her! Just shut that bird up! I can't take it anymore!"

* * *

Thanks for sticking around. They sometimes make me take breaks like that. You understand. But I wanted to finish, to tell you the two things they got wrong.

First, that mess about the affair. Some of the reports said that Leslie and Warren were not seeing each other romantically. Can you believe that? I mean, I was there. I saw it for myself. That business about her meeting with

him to pick up a first edition London she had him hunt up was a bunch of
baloney. Sure, they supposedly found that book in the trunk of her car, but
do you buy that?
What? Well, yeah, our anniversary was the following week, but that was
just an excuse. Todd must have somehow planted that book to cover for his
cheating sister. It's so obvious.
   Then there's that story about Mr. Harry. Is that a piece of fiction or what?
How do they come up with that stuff, saying I broke his neck the same night
I killed that adulteress? That is the flimsiest story they've come up with yet!
If I had killed Mr. Harry the night I strangled that cheater, how could he have
started squawking the next night while the police were interviewing me, huh?
Answer me that?
   Dead! Can you believe that?
   Oh, sure, they'll tell you how that officer walked over to the cage that night
of my confession and pulled off the cover only to find that Mr. Harry was
dead. They might even show you some official-looking coroner's report, but
it's all a scam. You know as well as I do—
   There! Did you hear him? Don't pretend you didn't. I saw you flinch.
You heard him, because he's alive. Mr. Harry's alive. He's here. He sits in
the trees outside the windows. He screams those words—my words—over
and over. Sometimes he gets in. He's tormenting me. He's tormenting me
with those words. I wish he would stop. I wish they would make him stop!